"SING ME A DEATH SONG"

——— A SPLATTER WESTERN ———

ROBERT ESSIG

DEATH'S HEAD PRESS

Published by Death's Head Press,
an imprint of Dead Sky Publishing, LLC
Miami Beach, Florida
www.deadskypublishing.com

Cover by Luke Spooner

Illustration by Mike Fiorentino, Jr.

Edited by Zoe Lemmon

CHAPTER ONE

NEWS GETS 'ROUND

NEWS TRAVELS SLOW ACROSS countless miles of dusty plateaus and desolate hills. Travels about as fast as a stagecoach can ride or a horse can gallop, that is if the rider doesn't run into trouble on the way. News dies then.

It was in some dusty nowhere town that Blue heard news that his momma's ranch had been seized by a group of marauders.

"Son of a bitch," Blue said as he sat at a table in the back of the saloon, puffing on a cigarillo. He preferred them when he could smoke them, but more often rolled his own using whatever cheap tobacco he could procure. If ever he befriended a bandido, he was sure to bargain for a batch of good cigarillos.

Watson Billings was the man sitting at a rickety old table with Blue, as nervous as a fat chicken in a meat market. He'd come from La Plateau, fresh off a weeklong ride north for reasons he was reluctant to discuss. Stopped in to wet his whistle, saw Blue in the shadows and plopped himself down to share the bad news. In a place such as this one wary eyes followed each new face, but people kept to their own table. This was not a saloon of upbeat music and laughter so much as a place of serious gambling and drinking.

"Who are they?" Blue asked.

Watson shook his head. "I don't know, Blue. But they have it in for you. Word is they're waiting for you to come back."

Blue nodded, glanced across the room at the barkeep tending to customers seated at the bar. "Figures. How about Blake and Pappy Cort? Them's my ranch hands. Any word on them?"

Watson shook his head. "I really don't know nothin'. I was just passing through, heard word, knew it was your momma's ranch."

Blue took a deep drag and blew the smoke into the already smoky air of the saloon. "My ranch now, but it'll forever be known as my momma's ranch."

Watson nodded. "Yessir it will. Your momma was a fine woman. She really was."

"A firecracker, some would say. Rollin' in her grave at thought of some goddamned marauders taking over her place."

On the table stood a bottle of whiskey and a pair of shot glasses. The bottle was old and cloudy looking. The whiskey was cheap, but Blue liked it that way. No use paying for the good stuff that didn't make his guts burn. He never drank much anyway. Just enough to keep his senses sharp. Just in case he had to reach for his gun. He scanned the room again, glancing at the patrons talking and dealing cards, as he'd been doing since he took a seat at a table against the back wall where the light from the kerosine lanterns was faint. He'd seen the looks on so many grisly faces as he walked in. Shifty eyes sizing up another such wanderer. Some folks had a gleam of recognition, perhaps a hope that Blue didn't have their wanted poster in his possession.

Blue leaned back, tilted his head and looked Watson in the eyes as if trying to read the man's intentions. Had he been sent here to lead Blue back to his momma's ranch? Was he working for the folks who had commandeered the ranch?

Blue had killed men for far less.

Watson began trembling as if the hot air in the saloon dropped thirty degrees. Sweat beaded on his baldhead like dew on a watermelon. He eyes the whiskey and licked his lips.

Blue held that stare for a bit longer than necessary.

Keep 'em scared for their life. Keep 'em on their toes. The words swam in Blue's mind. Something Pappy Cort used to say, though the man had never killed anyone in his entire life. It was just a way of intimidating people in hopes that he would never have to pull a six-shooter. Cort had enjoyed the drinking establishments in La Plateau, but he was no gunslinger. He was like a father to Blue after his real father was fatally injured by an ornery bull. Blue was too young to remember. The story was that his pa had been gored in the stomach so bad his insides were showing. Momma shot the bull, figuring it had gone mad. All he knew of his real father were in the form of stories from his mother and a detailed drawing of the man. Pappy Cort had helped Blue's mother by taking on greater responsibilities at the ranch. Over the years he'd taught Blue a lot about life, the things he figured a mother couldn't rightly reach a young boy. How to shoot a gun, how to gut an animal. Eventually he taught Blue how to drink and most importantly, how to treat women with respect, a trait Cort felt too many cowboys lacked.

After pouring two shots, Blue slid one across the table. "Have a drink with me."

Watson nodded and let out a breath he must have been holding through the entire duration Blue had stared him down. He smiled and nodded. "Pleased to have a drink with you, Blue."

"I'm not pleased to get the bad medicine, but I'm glad you filled me in. I was going to head east tonight, but that's done changed."

"What's waiting for you out east?"

Blue's eyes shot up at Watson with a clear message not to ask questions that don't pertain to him. There were stories about Blue Covington in just about every town in the west, and even into the east. Watson knew enough to assume some things were fabricated, but he didn't know where the truth ended and the fable began. Blue was a bounty hunter, but some folks claimed he worked dirty. Problem was, most folks who were on the wrong side of the law made false accusations in defense of their own poor judgment.

Watson nodded. "Sorry," he stammered out the words, "none of my business."

"It ain't." Blue poured himself another shot of rotgut. Sipped it. "So tell me, Watson Billings, why this bodega? You're not the type I thought would frequent a bucket of blood like this one."

Watson got to shaking again. Around him patrons talked and glasses clinked. The overpowering reek of body odor and stale beer cut through the acrid smoke. "Well, I, uh," he licked his lips. "I was just looking for a place to get a drink." A nervous chuckle.

"You're a piss poor liar, you know that? Good thing you never took up poker."

"Really, Blue," trembling, Watson shook his head fervently. "Blue, you got to—"

"What'd they pay you to track me down?"

"I swear—"

Blue's right hand swung down and grabbed his revolver from its holster at unnatural speed, the gun pulled and pointed at Watson's head before he could stammer out another broken word. Blue pulled back the hammer and cocked the gun. Hardly anyone looked their way, as if used to such outbursts, though talk hushed some.

"You didn't come in here for a drink, you lying bag of mule shit." Blue pulled back the hammer and cocked the gun. "I'm no dummy. I have myself positioned back here where no one can get a good look at me. Finding me here ain't no accident."

Watson licked his lips and swallowed hard. His jaw trembled.

Blue smiled and let out a gargle of laughter. "You came looking for me. How much they pay you? They certainly didn't send you here to kill me. You don't have the balls." As he spoke he shot a quick glance to the entrance of the saloon as someone walked in, before barreling his eyes back into Watson's. "You really are a spineless piece of shit, aren't you?"

As Watson froze in his shivering state, Blue continued his surveillance of the bodega. He had already been waiting for someone before Watson joined his table.

"Look here. You let me know how much they paid you, and you might leave alive." Blue spit in his face. "Might."

Blue looked up again. His eyes narrowed as he gazed longingly at the bar. Watson didn't dare turn to see who had caught Blue's attention.

"Well," Blue said, "you got about thirty seconds to tell me what I need to know, because the man I've been waiting for has just entered the saloon and is at the bar getting himself a drink." Watson shifted as if to turn and see who this man was. "No. Don't you dare turn around on me. How much did they pay you? I already know I'm heading back to La Plateau. It's just a matter of whether I'm killing one man or two right now."

Watson, trembling, said, "Two hundred."

Blue tilted his head, his brow contorting. His eyes darted to the man behind Watson, his unshielded form standing at the bar. He held his cocked gun to the side of Watson's head. "You better duck or your ears'll be ringin' like hell."

Gritting his teeth and squinting one eye, Blue took aim. Watson dropped to the floor just as the six-shooter made a deafening pop. Just one shot. The crowd gasped, glasses clinking, followed by a brief moment of silence after several women screamed. A few folks ushered themselves outside and away from the violence. The regulars resumed drinking and dealing cards, chuckling and thankful they weren't a part of the outburst.

The man who'd been shot in the back of the head hesitated before falling to the floor. Behind the fallen corpse, the bartender was awash in the blood that sprayed from the exploding exit wound. Blue hadn't been concerned with the aftermath. He never was while taking down wanted men. He learned a while back that using his knife to score an X on the tip of his bullets met with horrendous results that insured a kill. Some folks got shot in the head and had enough instincts about them to reach for their own gun and fire back. With a notched bullet their brains always blew out the exit wound. That poor bastard bartender just happened to be in the wrong place at the wrong time.

Gesturing to Watson, who was crouched on the floor, Blue said, "Come on."

The bartender was flicking bloody chunks out of his eyes when Blue and Watson approached the lifeless body on the floor. The din resumed moments after the killing. With some excitement, the scarred and dust blown faces had something to talk about while getting drunk, before the next fight inevitably broke out. Behind the bar there were notches in the wood that once represented each person who had been killed over a bad game of Faro, a lover's triangle, a wanted man, or any other reason for someone to shoot first and keeps questions to themselves. The bartender who started notching the wood was shot one night when a rowdy individual took offense to him always notching when the man killed someone. It was petty, but then again so many murders in a place like this could have been resolved more peacefully by men with straighter heads.

The bartender used a dirty rag to wipe brains and blood from his face. Blue regarded him, feeling genuinely sorry for the man. It was never Blue's intention to put anyone else in danger while getting a bounty. Or to splatter a head full of gore on another man like this.

"I do apologize," Blue said to the bartender. "I should have given you a sign or something." Blue slapped down several coins. "For the drink and your troubles. The guy here, we're taking him out. Ain't no one gonna know him from his face, but he's got other markings on him. Scars and such."

The bartender slid the money off the counter into his waiting hand, then deposited it in some kind of locked box beneath the bar. He didn't even count it. Didn't have to. Blue had given him a handsome tip.

"Grab him," Blue said to Watson.

"Me?"

"Well yeah, who else?"

"But—"

"Just grab his feet and drag the son of a bitch out of here."

Watson, confused and wary of the look in Blue's eyes, dragged the man out of the saloon. Patrons cleared a path, eyeing the dead man with piteous smirks. Once outside Blue asked, "Which one's your horse?"

"The black Morgan, second from the left."

Blue nodded. "That's a nice ride there. Hope she can afford the extra weight."

"Extra weight?"

"I like you, Watson." Blue smirked. "That you came lookin' for me either shows that you're dumb, brave, or stupid. You take this bounty north to Tennessee. He's worth five hundred dead or alive. You don't say a word to anyone you found me, hear?"

Watson nodded and slumped his shoulders. He glanced at the body, grimaced, and quickly looked away, his eyes darting to anything but the corpse.

Blue shook his head. "Hate to say it, but I don't think bravery brought you out here."

Blue approached his Saddlebred mare, clicked a few times to let her know they were about to depart, then undid the rope from the hitching rail.

"How am I supposed to get him up on the horse?" Watson asked.

"You'll figure it out. He's worth a good bounty, so watch yourself. Some other bounty hunter will shoot you between the eyes for that there man. No one will know who he is so long as they don't see his scars. Travel by night, due east. Follow the moon. I hear you spoke even one word about running into me, I'll find you and next time I won't be quite so generous."

Blue leapt upon his horse and rode off west, toward La Plateau.

CHAPTER TWO

MEANWHILE, BACK IN LA PLATEAU

LOUISE CAMPBELL WATCHED THE show from the back of the Mid Town Saloon, alone at a small table amongst the townsfolk. The place was lit by large kerosine lamps, which gave an almost ethereal quality, especially in the back where Louise preferred to sit. Most of the lamps were positioned around the stage to provide the audience a better view of the performers. There were a few card tables with their own lamps and a bar that bustled with local gossip and tall tales from lonely rovers in between the evening acts on stage.

Some folks didn't think it was ladylike to attend a variety show alone, but Louise didn't give a good goddamn what anyone said or thought about her demeanor. On the contrary, many people in town cared a great deal about what she said and thought, and therefore people generally left her alone even though she often went against the grain. Her coming to La Plateau in the first place had been a move that most women of the west would have been terrified to make alone, especially at the age of fifteen. That was damn near twenty years ago. She'd fled her home town in Kentucky after her grandmother was hanged for practicing black magic, but it wasn't that at all. It was a gift. One that Louise inherited. When those holy rollers came after the rest of Louise's family, they fled. She was the only one with the gift, and fearing for their safety in her presence, she tucked her hair into a hat, donned cowboy duds, and headed west alone.

When she came upon La Plateau, she felt a kinship with the people. They were kind and generous and greeted her with open arms. She dropped the rugged facade she'd been hiding behind while traveling and settled down. Eventually she gained enough trust to share her gift with the locals, being sure to do it in a way that wouldn't result in her dangling from a tree like her grandmother, God rest her soul.

On stage the Bridgeford Trio belted out a song with pithy lyrics that had an almost comical sense. Their music was a blend of cowboy ranch tunes, traditional standards, and something that was uniquely Bridgeford Trio, something Louise couldn't put her gloved finger on. They'd been in town all week, playing in the variety show that Mid Town Saloon put on almost nightly. The cowboys watched for the dance hall girls. The dancers wore big fluffy dresses, but when they danced in a line and kicked their legs up high the audience was given an eyeful. The younger cowboys had never seen so much leg. Some of them got all horned up and visited the brothel upstairs afterward, and even more of them were foolish enough to think the dancing line girls were up there waiting for them.

The musical acts that played the variety show usually stayed for a few weeks and then moved onto the next town. They were paid by the saloon, and often pumped the strings of a guitar or blew a harmonica throughout the day out on Main Street with a top hat or guitar case upturned at their feet, hoping for small coins from folks who enjoyed a little serenade. The Bridgeford Trio were no different. They had a guitar player, a harmonica player, and a fiddle player. All of them sang, and their voices blended like rich cream, soothing to the ears, though their choice of lyrics were often absurd and odd, which would in turn cause certain members of the audience to heckle in between songs, yearning to hear a tried and true standard, something the whole place could sing with. Something about camptown ladies doo dah, doo dah.

Louise sipped a brandy as she watched them play, curious what their hands would tell her. Considering the trouble they'd been causing, she figured their palms would be a fascinating read were she given the opportunity. Her profession was one of near secrecy, considering how judgemental people could be, what with palmistry not being very Christian and all. Little did the townsfolk know that their very own preacher had been to visit Louise in a weak moment, struggling with his beliefs.

Will, the fiddle player, did most of the solo singing, with the other two joining in for chorus lines or backing vocals. When Will sang he made exaggerated facial gestures after certain lyrics. Louise didn't find them all that amusing, and neither did the rest of the audience, which had grown since the Bridgeford Trio started playing the saloon a week prior. People didn't come for the music, per say.

They came to see who would get a death song.

It started five days ago with a heckler in the audience. There was always one. The Bridgeford Trio had gone through their various renditions, smiling and playing their songs. Peaceful, jolly men who appeared as harmless as a tailor in church. That first night they soured at the words of the heckler. The final song came with horrendous lyrics so violent that the audience was left in awe. When the very man who had stood and jeered was found dead the following morning, no one suspected the Bridgeford Trio. But each night someone did something to disrupt the show. An outburst of laughter caused a second person to die brutally in their sleep. Then it was a fellow who stumbled drunk into a table and caused several mugs to shatter on the floor. The singing group smiled as they sang those awful songs, and soon enough people began to put the pieces together, blaming the Bridgeford Trio for the deaths. No one could make sense of how each person was being murdered so violently in their sleep, but the morning revelations were undeniable.

On the tail end notes of an original tune they called "Cattle Driving Ladies" a man in the audience lobbed a remark. "You couldn't carry a tune in a bucket!" So original. They were fine singers, the man was just trying to get under their skin. The crowd collectively gasped, for they knew this was a fatal mistake.

Will, leader of the group, tilted his head and squinted his eyes, searching the smoky room for the man who dared heckle. Five days into their stay and the people of La Plateau should be well aware that heckling the Bridgeford Trio was a very bad idea indeed. A few days ago the local grocer had merely made a critical comment about their performance, suggesting that the night would have been better served by another dance routine from the line girls. The Brigeford Trio took the comment to heart, dedicating their next song to the heckler. Not only was he found dead the next morning, he'd died exactly the way their lyrics predicted.

"It was me!" The man stood proud. "Ain't no cattle driving ladies I ever heard of! You don't know what the hell you're singing about. Maybe go on back north where you come from. You can't fool *real* cowboys with those cheap lyrics. Good for nothin' no nothin' idiots!"

Will raised his eyebrows exaggeratedly. "Well well. Has your mother ever told you if you have nothing good to say, don't say anything at all? Maybe not in a town like this, but where I come from we were taught manners."

Rojo, the guitar player, strummed a couple of chords, punctuating his leader's sentiment, to which a few members of the crowd began to clap. Their joy was soon stifled at the leering eyes of fellow townsfolk who better shared the opinion of the outspoken man who now stood so everyone could see him clearer. He was a bold son of a bitch.

"You half breed!" The man pointed at Rojo. "You ain't welcome here. Go on back where you come from."

Will smiled, pivoted his head toward Rojo. "You believe this guy? Calling you a half breed, and I'm pretty sure you's as Mexican as they come."

Rojo said, "It's probably because I speak English better than some of these . . ." he trailed off.

"Some of these what?" the man in the audience said.

Louise knew what was coming just as well as everyone else, and there was nothing she could do about it. The man standing up was Harold Strummer. A well-seasoned cowboy who tended to drink too much and run his mouth. Louise knew Harold's deepest secrets, as she did so many others in town. He'd come to visit her once. She grabbed his grungy hands and saw everything. The abuse. The blackout drinking. His own father and uncle beating and raping him. She saw it all and saw clearly how the man became such a bitter specimen of human offal. Somehow his wife stuck by his side through the beatings and verbal abuse. Had his wife been here she probably would have remained silent, even though she, like everyone else in the audience, knew perfectly well that Harold was signing his own death certificate.

"Well, folks," Will said. "Looks like we're going to sing our last song for the night. I really hoped we could make it through a set without one of these renditions, but as you can see, some folks just can't keep their mouths shut."

Harold started up again, his voice slurred and impassioned, but Will spoke over him.

"Here's another death song to cap off what was otherwise a delightful night," Will nodded at his fellow players, and they started up the familiar tune. It was in a minor key, which gave it an awfully spooky sound that unnerved the audience, an audience who wanted terribly to do something, but were afraid that a death song would be coming their way if they did. Men clutched guns that rested in holsters, dreaming of firing a bullet through any one of their three faces, but what if they missed? What if they only got one of them? Would the other two sing a death song for their wife or children in revenge?

Whispers in hushed tones too low to battle the singing expressed familiar concerns throughout the crowd, followed by gasps and nervous coughs as Will sung the final line, ". . . ignorant brains seeping from Harold's ears, a hundred stab wounds take away all his fears . . ."

Low murmurings began around the saloon.

"Someone's has *got* to do something about this."

"We can't live in fear."

"They need to be hung by their necks 'til they're dead."

"A bullet in the head'll do mighty fine."

When the Bridgeford Trio finished the death song, they promptly bowed to a silent audience. The murmurs would not dare be spoken any louder for fear they would unleash another killing tune, not that anyone had ever seen them perform that song twice in a night. They walked off stage and exited through a door just beyond an open area backstage where performers could ready themselves before a show.

Louise watched as the town's sheriff, Grover Davis, stood from a table in the middle of the saloon and hurried upstairs for a better view from a window in one of the working ladies' rooms above. He returned a couple minutes later.

"They're down the road toward the hotel where they're staying," Sheriff Davis announced.

At this, the room opened up to a boisterous conversation. Talk of murdering the musicians, to which Sheriff Davis discouraged.

"Then why don't you do something, Sheriff?" someone asked. "Poor Harold is gonna wake up dead, I just know it. And then what?"

"Maybe we should stop coming here watching them," Sheriff Davis suggested. "How about that? Maybe they'll just go away."

"They've killed five so far. Harold will be number six. And still there ain't no justice. That's on you, Sheriff."

Harold said, "I'm not dying in my sleep. That's bullshit." Not looking very convinced, he tipped back a bottle of whiskey that had mysteriously been placed on his table—an offering for a dead man walking.

"We don't know they killed anybody," someone said.

"The hell we don't!" The town coroner had been the one who started putting the pieces together, he and Sheriff Davis being the only two who had closely examined each victim. "It's in the words. They say things in them songs, terrible things. I seen the aftermath just the other day. It ain't natural to die that way in one's sleep is all I'm saying."

"Why haven't they gone?" someone asked.

All eyes shifted to Frenchy Hill, the bartender and owner of Mid Town Saloon. Frenchy was a staple of La Plateau. Everyone knew him. People trusted him. He'd become a sort of confidante, being the man who served the beer and poured the shorts. He may not have known the deeper secrets that Louise knew, but he knew everything else that went on in town.

Frenchy's face tightened. "I haven't paid them." Gasps and rising murmurs. Frenchy's voice rose, "I haven't paid them because of what they've been doing. They don't deserve it."

"Well why the hell do you allow them to get up there and sing every night?" the coroner asked.

Frenchy raised his eyebrows. "You're telling me if you were in my boots you'd kick them out? I don't need no one in my family dying in their sleep, God damn it. And I ain't paying a bunch of low down murderers either." Frenchy shifted his gaze to Sheriff Davis, leveling a telling sneer.

The rumblings increased. Finally Sheriff Davis yielded to their insistence. "Okay," he resigned, "Okay. I'll round them up in the morning." His eyes traced the patrons looking to him for answers. "It seems our morbid curiosity does nothing more than bring us here every night to see who's next. I believe in justice and law, but I also believe a community can come together to fix their own problems. We're all scared of them. We're all scared we'll be next." He nodded and took a deep breath. "I suppose it's in my job title to be the one who takes care of this."

The dull thud of a glass smacking one of the old tables silenced the room. It was Cort "Pappy" Rudgers, an old timer in town who'd been working the Covington Ranch for the past twenty years.

"Them's killers right there. Three of 'em. This isn't a problem for townsfolk to care after. This is a problem for the law, but it seems the law hasn't been doing its job lately. I haven't seen a goddamn thing done about Covington Ranch. Me an' Blake Martin are out of work, and . . . aw hell, I don't even know what happened to Ed Long. There hasn't been so much as an investigation up there. It's like you just let them marauders have the land." Pappy shook his head.

"People are starting to leave town," someone said, and then the din of concerned argument erupted once again. Pappy hung his head and wept. Seemed no one gave a damn about Covington Ranch, not while the Bridgeford Trio were in town killing people.

Louise slipped off her gloves and crossed the room to where Pappy sat. She pulled up a chair beside him, steadied herself, and put her hands on his. His head shot up, and when he saw who was comforting him, there was a look of terror that came over him. Louise had her eyes closed, reading deeply of what her gift showed her. Though Pappy was fearful of the woman in town who could read fortunes, he was also smitten with the touch of her soft hands, the delicate nature of her features that made her look almost like one of those porcelain dolls he'd seen once when a caravan of Chinese immigrants came through town selling goods.

She twitched, jaw clenching, a pained expression tattooed across her face. Deep breathed through her nose, and then she steadied. Louise opened her eyes. She looked troubled, her gift telling her he didn't have much time. "I'm not so sure about the future of Covington Ranch."

Pappy shook his head. "That ranch was all I got. I'm lost without it."

Pulling her gloves back on, Louise said, "I apologize. Maybe I shouldn't have done that. Sometimes I," she hesitated, wary. "I don't like what I see."

Pappy looked up, eyes grave, and nodded as if accepting a dire fate. He looked very old at that moment, older than he was. His hair was thin and gray and his beard only had hints of color. He was skinny, but toned and more willing to put in a hard day's work than a lot of the younger folks in town.

"Excuse me."

Louise turned to see Sheriff Davis standing there. "Yes, Sheriff?"

"Could I have a word with you? In private."

She thought on it for a moment too long, wishing she didn't have to touch the sheriff's hand to see his true intentions. "Why sure." She offered a courteous smile, bid Pappy goodnight, and walked outside, Sheriff Davis in tow.

CHAPTER THREE

THE MARAUDERS

EDWIN "FULL SPLIT" GROVER aimed his pistol and fired off another round into the cow's face, cackling as he did so. He enjoyed shooting his gun, but especially enjoyed shooting living things. Animals. People. The first shot was the best. It had taken the bovine down. The thud it made when it hit ground was magnificent, and caused the beast to evacuate its bowels on impact, which Edwin thought was spectacular. He'd have liked for it to have stayed upright so he could have target practice, but decided to fire off more rounds into its face on the ground. At least until the thing's legs stopped kicking.

Once the cow stopped kicking in the grips of its death throes, Edwin reloaded his revolver and holstered it, pondering death. It was so easy to put a bullet in something's head. So easy to play the part of the Grim Reaper. But Edwin wasn't grim about it. He was more of a Gleeful Reaper. Killing brought him joy. Made his twig and berries feel all warm a fuzzy. He looked over his shoulder toward the ranch house, longing for the woman inside to be standing there all hot and bothered, as if she'd been watching him kill the cow and got all turned on. He knew killing didn't do it for her like it did him. She was ruthless, but it was more like a business transaction when she pulled a pistol, and rarely did she do that. She'd have Edwin pull his, which he right appreciated.

The gunfire had startled the herd, scattering them across the pasture. Edwin lifted his revolver once again and took aim, but they were too far away. He'd have to get his rifle if he wanted some fun. Instead he walked over to the fire pit and pulled a slender tree branch that had been protruding from the tangle of blackened bones and ash. He walked around to the back of the ranch home where the corpses of three cattle were laid out on the ground in various stages of rot. He went to the largest one and used the blackened end of the branch to draw a series of circles. At the center of the circles he made a small black dot, but was careful not to apply too much pressure. He could feel the give from the cow's soft, dead flesh. It was so filled with death gasses it was fit to burst.

Standing back enough paces for a proper showdown, Edwin stood for a moment, right hand at his side, hovering over his holstered revolver. He'd never been in a showdown before, but he'd seen plenty of them growing up. He'd watch from the window of the little room his mother would hide him in when she had a customer, what she would call a gentleman friend. He didn't mind being banished to the little room because there was a window and a chair. Little Edwin would stand on the chair and watch the town, and what a rough place it was. He'd seen many a showdown from that little room. Seen men rob, cheat and steal. Saw a lot of bloodshed. Saw things people thought no one could see, all while listening to grunting and moaning and thumping that he misinterpreted as so many different things that his ragged ol' momma could have been doing with her gentlemen friends, all of which was inaccurate as he finally found out one day when he'd decided he had enough of living half his life locked up in a closet.

Edwin had drifted off again, and like so many other times when he drifted off, he drifted back to that god-damned little room. He'd lived his life as a drifter, often finding solace in sleeping under the stars. From time to time he would start to thinking, and his mind would end up in that room again, listening to his mother fuck her dusty old cowboys and traveling outlaws.

Making a sudden and quick grab for his gun, Edwin pulled the revolver and shot like he was in a duel and his life depended on accuracy. He didn't even hit the bloated animal.

After a few deep breaths to calm himself, he took proper aim at the center of the bullseye and pulled off another shot. This one hit true center and he was rewarded with more than a mere bullet hole in a dead animal, but something extraordinary. The puncture was small, but the death gasses were built up and the release was too much for the tender, rotten flesh. The hole blew open outward like the thing had been blasted with a shotgun from the inside, flowering rotten, slimy flesh out in a vile bloom that caused Edwin to jump back a few steps as not to get sprinkled in putrid gore.

It happened quickly, a loud pop from the gun and then another pop from the bloated bovine. It lay there sunken in on itself in a pool of wet decomposition. Edwin stood and watched as the rotten guts writhed with thousands of maggots. He'd never seen anything like this from the little window in his mother's secret room.

James Salmon was a nervous man with a genius brain that rarely met its full potential, especially since he met Minnie Granger a few short years ago. He'd been dedicated to his studies back when they met, but grew tired of the repetitious nature of higher education. He excelled in geometry and logic, but found there was no room for creativity in college. Precise mimicry of the lessons was required, as if the students were rewarded for imitation rather than innovation.

He hadn't been one of those men who chased after women and settled for a working lady when he found himself looking at the foamy bottom of an empty beer mug. There was something about Minnie that had him hooked from the first sight. He wasn't even sure it was love. It was something he couldn't describe, which was strange for a man as learned as James Salmon. If there was one thing he didn't learn in college, it was studies in the nature of women.

Invading the Covington Ranch had been nerve-wracking for James. He and Minnie had planned bank robberies that went off without a hitch, mostly due to James' smarts. He'd outlined detailed schemes that pulled in riches and most often didn't require harm to anyone. It was so easy to just kill and steal, but that also led to warrants and bounties. James had planned heists in a way that left no clues as to how it was the money had disappeared. That was the key to their success over the past couple years. Well, for he and Minnie. Edwin was another story. James didn't care all that much for Edwin, but on the other hand James was no marksman. He tried his hand at shooting, but it just wasn't in him. He felt awful that he wouldn't be able to protect Minnie, not that she needed a man to protect her. If it weren't for her sultry femininity, she could have cut her hair off and been taken for the opposite sex. She was that brazen, that foul mouthed, and more confident than just about any woman James had ever encountered. Those were the things, along with her long, dark curled hair and full lips, that attracted him to her. Frankly, Minnie had all of the qualities women looked for in a man that James lacked.

There was also that thing she did with her mouth that even the ladies of the night weren't likely to agree to. James hadn't been one who was concerned with his libido, not until Minnie came into his life. When he was fourteen he visited one of the whorehouses on the edge of Cincinnati, where he grew up. The place was notorious, especially for young boys who were looking to become men but couldn't find a girl who'd have a roll in the hay. James, along with two friends, had gone to that seedy little village across the train tracks. They'd saved up some coins and decided that they would all become men that day. James, being apprehensive about the whole thing, wasn't nearly as eager as his cohorts. The woman who agreed to bed with the boys one by one wasn't particularly attractive, but took on the challenge with vigor. James was last to have a go, and by then she was worn and haggard. The smile she had offered the boys when they arrived was replaced with a weary grimace. She hadn't done more cleaning that a mere wipe with a rag between each of his friends, which made for an entirely unpleasant experience for James. When he couldn't come to climax and went limp inside the woman, she laughed at him. He was so embarrassed by the experience that he lied to his friends about what had happened.

James had lived a virginal life until the day he crossed Minnie's path. Whenever he thought of bedding down with a woman he could hear that old whore laugh. Could smell the musty odor of her quarters. But Minnie was so unlike her. Minnie took care of herself. She wore fragrances that were imported from France. She painted her face up when she went out. She was clean.

With a washrag and a basin of water, James cleaned himself before buttoning his trousers. Minnie glared at him, having seen him perform this act after every sexual encounter they had.

"Is my mouth so disgusting that you have to use a clean cloth and water on your pecker like that?"

James looked up. Minnie's face was hitched up and her eyes afire. James felt an immediate shame, something too easily stirred up from that awful day he attempted to lose his virginity to the sweaty old whore.

He stammered, "I, uh, well, you see—"

"You think sex is such a dirty thing, do you?"

James shook his head.

"Well, how would you feel if I stopped doing that thing, huh? I bet you wouldn't like that, now would you?"

He shook his head even more.

Minnie smiled. "I didn't think so. You know, James, most ladies won't stick that thing in their mouth like I do, but when I see you getting to worrying and fretting, well, it's one thing I know will get you to calm down a bit. Is that right? Does that help calm your nerves?"

"Well, yes, I suppose it does." James bowed his head, shamefully bashful even in the presence of the woman he loved, the woman who would grant his every sexual desire, no matter how few they really were. "It's just, I don't rightly know what we're doing out here. La Plateau isn't a rich town. We haven't been planning a heist here. I . . ." His voice wavered. "Someone was killed. We haven't killed anybody yet."

A gunshot echoed from outside, followed by a whooping sound from Edwin.

James lowered his voice. "That man out there is a loose cannon."

"Aw, he's not so bad. We need a man like that around," Minnie cooed. "Besides, I'll have you know that I have complete control over this situation. What we're doing here has everything to do with honoring my family." Her smile dropped. "You wouldn't want to get in the way of that, now would you?"

"No, ma'am."

"Oh cut it out with the ma'am shit, James. I ain't your mother. I just done suckled your pecker like a hungry calf." Minnie shook her head. "Sometime I swear, James, all that learning you did pushed common sense right out of your head. Look here, I want Mr. Blue Covington dead. Simple as that. That's why we're here. That's also why Edwin is here. You might have the brains, but one thing God didn't instill in you is the brawn."

Minnie extended her hand toward James, placing her finger on his chin. She spoke in a sultry voice. "Every man has it in him, I'm sure of it. You just have to find it. You can show me that you tough, that you can fight, well, there wouldn't be no need for Edwin 'round here."

She kissed James on the lips. Not so much sensual as it was a peck to punctuate her statement. He did everything in his power not to shiver in horror and spit profusely, considering she hadn't washed out her mouth after sucking him off.

Minnie walked out of the room. James felt a strange mix of emotions. He liked what she did with her mouth. Not as much as he liked bedding with her, but it certainly did calm him down. The woman was crass, and that bothered him at times, but over the past two years he'd pretty much warmed up to her ways. And yet she could say something so distasteful that James actually wanted to slap her across the face, not that he would ever do such a thing. The men in his family were proper and wouldn't dare allow a woman to speak so openly. James had found her brazenness equally offensive and strangely alluring, in an exotic sort of way.

James could hear Minnie's voice outside as she talked to Edwin. James hated Edwin. Just like he had the urge, at times, to slap that filthy mouth on Minnie, he wanted to put a bullet in Edwin's face.

Chapter Four

They Sung Me a Death Song

Harold Strummer stumbled home from the saloon. He'd stayed after the Bridgeford Trio sung him his fate. There was talk of hanging them with or without the law's consent. Some people said the musicians needed to be burned. By the time Harold left, old friends and acquaintances were saying their goodbyes like he wasn't going to be back. He said things like "don't be ridiculous!" and "ain't no queer black magic gonna do me in," but by the time he'd made it to his home a few ruddy blocks away, his mind had begun to implode.

Harold opened the door to a home he'd mostly built himself. His wife Martha sat in candlelight, sewing idly, as she did on nights when Harold went to the saloon. He'd always tell her not to stay up, but she always did. On this night he was pleased to see her.

The carefree attitude he'd left the saloon with had been replaced with abject terror.

"Martha, they sung me a death song."

Martha's jaw dropped. "They what?" She had a way of annunciating the H in words like what and white, especially in a fit of emotion.

Harold nodded. "They sure did. Sung it to me loud and proud up there on that stage. I said to the sheriff, why do you let them perform like that? Why don't you arrest them? I don't think the sheriff gives a damn."

Martha sighed and looked away, her bespectacled eyes drawn, worried. She put her sewing down on a table.

Martha said, "Sheriff Davis doesn't have any proof them's the ones killing people."

"Proof? *Proof?* They sing one of them songs and that person up and dies. Happens every damn night. It has to be them."

"It's a strange coincidence, some might say uncanny, but there's never any proof."

"Then who's doing it? Who's killing these folks who get a death song sung to them? I'd like to know, because they're coming after me tonight."

Martha dropped her voice. "I'll stay up all night. I can brew some coffee. There's a little bit of grounds left. I'll stay up, Harold."

Harold shook his head. "That don't matter none. I don't know how they do it, but they do it well. The other day it was Jackson Hubble. He's got a wife and three kids. They knew his fate. Marcy sat up all night in the living room, right beside the front door. All she had to do was pivot her head and she could see the back door. It squeaks whenever someone comes in. Dry hinges. I told Jackson a little rendered hog fat would do the trick to quiet them hinges, but . . ." Harold trailed off. "Anyway, she sat up all night. Thought they'd beat the curse or whatever it is. Went upstairs and—"

"I know what happened. No use'n repeatin' old news." Martha shuddered. "'Specially of that nature."

"My point is, there was no one got into that house that night, and yet Jackson was killed in his own bed." Harold stumbled, catching himself on a countertop in the kitchen. "And I'm next."

"What did you say to get them to single *you* out?"

"I just told them they couldn't sing worth a shit. That's pretty much what I said."

"Then why did you go in the first place? If they're so bad why does anybody go?"

"To see who gets the death song, I suppose."

Martha shook her head. "If half the town wasn't there every night, maybe they'd up and leave. Ever think about that?" Martha stood up and comforted her husband. "You're drunk is all. Here, let me help you to bed. I'll sit watch. Better than that, I'll come up and check on you every hour."

Harold looked Martha dead in the eyes. His eyelids were droopy, which was the sure sign that he'd drunk far too much and was on the verge of passing out. It was a look Martha hated, one she'd begun to know and understand. It was the reason she stayed up for him when he went to the saloon. She liked to make sure he made it home. One night a few years back she woke up to an empty bed, went out looking for him and found Harold halfway between the saloon and their house, nestled up in a chicken pen. She'd found him just as the Pendersons, owners of the chicken coop, did, and they were none too happy about it. Especially since one of the chickens was dead. Harold had been using it as a pillow. Martha had been so filled with shame that she'd never gone to sleep on saloon nights since.

Finally Harold succumbed to the tug of sleep that was already beginning to slow down his motor skills. He tripped up the stairs, Martha with her hands out, bracing him when he swayed backwards. After stripping down to his underclothes, he collapsed onto a feather mattress. Martha pulled a sheet up and tucked him in.

"I'm sorry," Harold said.

This caught Martha by surprise.

"Sorry? Whatever for?"

Harold took in a deep breath. "For all the bad things I've done. I haven't been as good to you as you deserve."

Martha pinched up her face in scrutiny. These were words she never thought she'd hear, even at his drunkest.

She patted his shoulder. "Don't worry about it, dear. Just get some sleep. In the morning all this nonsense will be over."

Louise lived very near the saloon in a building that housed a barber, a locksmith, and a spice seller. The door to her business and residence was located at the rear of the building, out of sight from the main street. If you weren't looking for it, you wouldn't know it exists. That's the way Louise liked it. That's the way the townsfolk liked it, for many of them were not only strict Christians (at least on Sundays and when they weren't at the saloon), but superstitious to boot. The idea of a palm reader was hard medicine to swallow, especially in a town like La Plateau. These were settlers building lives for themselves rather than treading west for unknown spoils, many of them second generation residents. With a local butcher, produce merchant, farm supply store, and a general store with enough connections to keep the shelves stocked with a wide variety of merchandise, they had everything they needed.

In the bigger cities, fortune tellers were much more welcome and able to advertise freely without judgment or suspicion, but Louise had found that La Plateau better accepted her when they could pretend that she did not exist. Out of sight, out of mind. She found that to be absurd, but in reality the judgmental nature of the town provided Louise with a great deal or privacy, which she enjoyed. She didn't want to end up an old spinster, but appreciated that she was able to manage herself freely without depending on the protection of a man.

At her door, Louise glanced at Sheriff Davis as he rounded the building. She smiled, watching his head dart this way and that, as if he were doing something wrong. Just about everyone in town had visited Louise on at least one occasion, and yet everyone acted as if she did not exist, professionally at least. They accepted her, for they knew she could see things others couldn't. In times of need they prayed, certainly, but they also had their palms read.

Louise opened the door. She waited for Sheriff Davis, offering a coy, knowing smile. He looked worried, but she could tell it wasn't about being seen with the palm reader. His worries were much deeper.

"Come, Sheriff," Louise said. "I know what you're thinking, but you should really be concerned about how it looks going into a woman's place at night like this, you know, you being married and all."

Sheriff Davis' face dropped. "But, but this is a place of—"

"Business? Yes. But nobody acknowledges that, now do they?" She shook her head. "Don't worry. Anyone sees you coming in here after what has been going on, they'll know why. And though they won't say it out loud, they'll appreciate the consultation. Come on in, let's get started."

Louise's parlor was a simple setup of a table surrounded by four chairs on one side of the room, and a sitting chair with a small end table and oil lamp on the other side. The walls were decorated with artistically arranged dried flowers and leaves, as well as various animal skulls. Morbid, and yet so gorgeously arranged that one didn't immediately think of Louise as a witch or some evil, godless woman who should be hanged. The room smelled of lavender mixed with the dying fragrance of so many decorative blooms hanging on the walls. Louise replaced them periodically, once the pleasant fragrance turned sour.

Louise used a match to light a stick from which she lit several oil lamps and candles. Sheriff Davis stood there for a moment examining the décor as the room became alight in a soft glow.

"Still got those damn skulls on the wall," he said.

"Sure I do. I change out the flowers often, but the skulls remain. If I ever find another, I'll add it."

"Get a lot of business?"

Louise shrugged. "Enough. I don't need a lot of business. I don't pay rent, I hardly have to pay for my foodstuffs. I have a little money tucked away, and enough to afford me the luxuries in life that I desire."

Sheriff Davis squinted his eyes. "Don't pay for rent? This building is on one of the most desirable locations in town."

"I barter."

Davis reared back in confusion, and then he understood.

"Look," he took a seat at the table. "I don't know how this is going to help, but at this point I'm at a loss for what to do."

"Sheriff, I know it's not my place to speak on such things, but those musicians are killers. I don't know how they do it, but it really is as plain as day."

"That's just it. I don't know how they do it either." David pinched the bridge of his nose, eyebrows furrowing. "What if they're merely suggesting things and someone else is doing the killing? I go and hang them musicians and there's still a killer out there in town somewhere. I just don't know what to do."

"Maybe take them in. The musicians. If they're locked up, they can't sing them songs. At least not in front of an audience where some killer is listening."

The sheriff ran a hand through his greasy hair. "But there'd still be a killer in town. How long until he kills again?" he shook his head. "I just don't know."

Louise sat down opposite of the sheriff. She began to remove her gloves, pulling one finger at a time. "Well, let me see your hand. Like I say to everyone who comes in, I'm no miracle worker, but I do see things. I may not be of help, sheriff, but I'd like to try."

Sheriff Davis pulled his hands back, his fingers wilting into untrusting claws. It had been quite some time since he'd been in Louise's abode. Last time he was there his daughter Martha was sick. The little girl had a raging fever, couldn't hold food down. The doctor was no help and the better doctors in nearby cities were too far away to get there in time. One evening Sheriff Davis found himself at the back of this very building, standing at the door that had a stylized hand painted on it. Louise was gentle with him, but he could see in her eyes that she saw his little girl dead. There was no way for Louise to hide it. She told him that his family would pull through. She was vague, but Sheriff Davis could see through her. Martha died a day later. As it turned out, Sheriff Davis didn't really want to know his daughter's fate, and yet Louise couldn't hide it from him.

"You're afraid I will see something bad like last time," Louise said.

Sheriff Davis said nothing.

"The way I do what I do is very tricky, Sheriff. I can't tell people everything I see. I have to navigate what I see in a way that is helpful. Some subjects are very hard to deal with. What you came in for last time, that was one of the most difficult palms I've had to read." Louise took in a deep breath and let it out. "Right now might be another very difficult palm. But I assure you, I will tell you," she hesitated for a split second, "everything."

Eyes locked on one another, Sheriff Davis hesitated as if seeking out Louise's true intentions, some ulterior motive he wasn't aware of. Or he was just plain scared. The truth could be hard to deal with, that he knew all too well.

He slid his hand across the table, and gave a little nod. "Go on now."

There was a twinkle in Louise's eyes. She wore the gloves every time she left her house just in case she were to have contact with anybody by mistake. Merely touching someone's hand would trigger her gift, and it was such a jolting shock when she was unprepared for it. While working, she took great pleasure in the thrill of traveling through another's mind via the touch of their flesh. It was like a drug. The look in her eyes was not unlike a drunk procuring a bottle of whiskey or an addict walking into an opium den.

Cradling the sheriff's hand in hers, Louise felt an immediate connection as if all the veins and nerve endings in his hand had extended from his fingers and wormed into Louise's skin, swimming into her veins and traveling through her body with each beat of her heart until she was fully consumed with the aura of Sheriff Davis. Eyes closed, Louise tilted her head back, contorted on her neck, her chest heaved out like she was having an episode, which, in a manner of speaking, she was.

Sheriff Davis sat there in that little room, inhaling the pleasant fragrance of lavender and watching as Louise's eyes darted left and right behind the thin fleshy lids. He'd seen this before, but his reaction was very much like someone who was experiencing their first palm reading.

Louise didn't say a word while she was traveling through the avenues of Sheriff Davis' mind. She was privy to seeing everything, and everything she saw. He had no terrible secrets to hide, nothing that she hadn't seen before. Like so many others, his life was fairly tragic.

Faces scream. Tears shed. Men shot dead. Ladies of the night giggle. His daughter lay dying. His wife crying. He puts a gun in his mouth. He drops it and it walks off, shooting a bullet through a wall in his house. He stumbles backwards, drunk.

She twitched, as she did when a memory or trauma was so intimate and telling, so shocking.

Sheriff Davis watched, his eyes deep caverns of desperate worry.

Navigating her way through the past, Louise began to see the future. In one's past the images were always clear. Even when the individual lived a life of drink the mind kept clear images of the life lived, as if the eyes were taking moving photographs that were locked in vast memory banks. Louise saw these moving pictures whenever she touched someone's hand. She saw them in vivid color and heard every excruciating sound, just as they played out in real life. But also, she could venture beyond memory and see other things. This is where it got sketchy. Memories were one thing, but seeing the future was another.

The streets of La Plateau strewn with bodies. Businesses closed down. The three musicians hang from nooses at the gallows. Their eyes gleam as if there is life in there, and smiles stretch across their faces like evil scarecrows.

Louise shuddered.

Sheriff Davis held in a breath. He inadvertently squeezed his hand and then Louise gripped it tighter.

In the distance, a fire spreads with the whipping winds across the plains, catching dry tumbleweeds that haven't been liberated from the desert floor. Fire that seems to be heading for La Plateau.

The hanged men laugh.

The fire intensifies, one dry bush after another until it hits Wilson Gabbard's carpentry business right on the edge of town. Deadwood coffins stacked three high become engulfed, and then the fire whips with the winds, licking the walls of the next building. The carpentry shop is an inferno. Wilson runs out and collapses on the ground amongst the dead, his body in flames.

Louise let go of Sheriff Davis' hand and drew hers back, as if she had suddenly become aware of some immediate threat. Her eyes opened, darting around the room wildly as the images she'd just lived through faded into her own memory banks and the dimly lit room took shape. Her breathing had accelerated, much more so than during the average reading. Putting her hands to her face, she was surprised to find that there were tears in her eyes.

Pulling his trembling hand back, Sheriff Davis whistled nervously. "That looked like a real wild ride, missy." He shook his head, reaching into a pocket on his vest and procuring a little tobacco pouch. He nodded at the pouch. "You mind?"

Louise shook her head. "Mind rolling one for me?"

"I'll roll and you talk."

She nodded, but remained quiet as he rolled the first cigarette. She watched his technique, admiring how graceful he made the act of rolling tobacco in a thin cut of paper appear. Also, she was trying to decipher the visions. Rarely were they so muted and cryptic. If what she'd seen was a clear indication of the future . . .

Sheriff Davis placed the freshly rolled cigarette before Louise, deliberately knocking on the table as he did so, to get her attention.

She grabbed the smoke and offered a weak grin. "Thank you." She put it in her mouth. Procuring a match, she waited until the sheriff had his smoke and then lit the match, lighting her cigarette, and then his. After a deep inhale, she said, "Hang 'em."

By candlelight, Martha stood watch over Harold into predawn. However she rationalized the situation, her fears had kept her awake for a while, but soon enough she was nodding off, nearly sliding from her chair and collapsing onto the floor. She decided to walk into the sitting room to stretch her legs. The sleepless night would be taxing on her come the morning sun, but it would be worth it to have her husband alive and well, no matter how much of a dirty dog he'd been in life. Maybe this experience would change him. He'd apologized just before falling asleep, after all. That in itself was something Martha never thought she would hear.

Deciding on coffee, Martha lit her stove and put on some water to boil. She'd locked the front and back doors before sitting in the little wooden chair beside the bed to watch over Harold. She checked the doors again. They both were still locked. It seemed so strange to lock the doors. She didn't really believe that those three musicians were going to sneak into their house and murder her husband, but she took the precaution anyway. She'd been close to a few townsfolk who had died mysteriously in their sleep. Though she hadn't seen their bodies with her own eyes, she'd been told how they were found. Her good friend Pearl was one such unfortunate. Found in bed withered away like a skeleton with her skin like dried beef. Faro games were never the same after Pearl died.

Just as the kettle whistled indicating that the water was boiling, another sound issued from upstairs. Martha rushed to the stove and pulled aside the kettle, concerned that the whistle had woken up Harold. A shrieking whistle like that in the dark of predawn would wake the dead.

The kettle cooled, the whistle fading fast, but the sound that came from upstairs, a low moaning and tortured sort of agony, remained.

It was Harold.

Martha grabbed a candle and took to the stairs, holding her flowing nightgown as not to trip over it and take a tumble. The low moaning came from the bedroom where Harold slept. She opened the door and entered, the candle illuminating the room in shaky light. A chill caused her to tighten her sleeping gown. The bed sheet was covering her husband, however spots of blood began appearing out of nowhere, spreading across the white linens. His eyes were closed, and yet his mouth was in a rictus of pain, teeth gritted tight.

Martha screamed, "Harold!"

He didn't wake up. The blood continued to spread. His body trembled beneath the sheet that was now saturated in deep red and sticking to his flesh like a new skin. Martha placed the candle on a small table beside the bed. She then grabbed a corner of the once white bed sheet and pulled it away from her husband's body, grimacing at the wet sound it made. The sheet felt like it had soaked up five pounds of blood. Martha let go and it dropped to the hardwood floor with a sickening splat. She closed her eyes and took a deep breath. Beneath Harold's body was a mess of shorn flesh as if someone had used a straight razor and shaved the skin off of him in tiny ribbons.

Martha screamed until she could scream no more, locked there in horror at what she witnessed. Tiny curls of flesh were spontaneously cut from his body. With each ribbon of curled flash that was skinned away from him, blood erupted, cascading over the sides of his torso, legs, and arms, and yet Harold didn't move. He twitched, as if trying to get away but unable to, as if his body was paralyzed, stuck in that moment to succumb to this sadistic fate without the ability to defend himself from his unseen attacker.

Martha's world went black. She collapsed on the floor and lay there unconscious as her husband was flayed, one strip of skin at a time, chest heaving, muscles trembling, until he died.

CHAPTER FIVE

SADDLEBAG REFLECTIONS

GROWING UP, BLUE NEVER thought he'd be a traveler. He thought he'd work his momma's ranch and one day take it over when she became too old and frail to carry on her duties. The idea of traveling across the country on horseback seemed wild and crazy. That was the type of thing lawless gunmen did. Traveling was for circuses and medicine shows, snake oil salesmen and people who were shunned or otherwise looking for a better life than the one they had wherever they had grown up.

Blue had always loved La Plateau. He loved his momma's ranch as well. On a good day he'd even say he loved the men momma had working there, Blake Martin and Cort "Pappy" Rudgers. On a good day. They were tough old bastards, but they were there for Blue after his daddy died. They became father figures, taught Blue a lot about life, and then Blue also taught himself a good deal. When Blue was a teenager, struggling with his hormones and the final tethers of childhood giving way to becoming a man, Cort took him aside several times, recognizing his struggle, and gave him words of encouragement. He often told him his father was watching from Heaven. Though Blue took comfort in that, he was also confused about Heaven and whether he believed in God at all.

The idea to settle down grew stale. Tending the ranch doing the same menial work day in and day out began to feel more like a fruitless task than a hopeful vision of the future. After managing to capture a couple of wanted men he'd spied traveling the trail alongside the ranch and being paid handsomely for their warrants, Blue developed an altruistic urge to clean up towns like La Plateau so people like his momma and ol' Pappy Cort could live in peace.

Only once he set out on what some folks in town called a "dead man's journey," he realized that his visions of being the savior of the west were misguided. He'd been looking for an escape from the repetitious work on the ranch. That was something he struggled with, something he'd never confessed to his momma for fear that it would break her heart. The ranch was all she'd ever known. It was what she'd lived for. How could he ever have told her his heart wasn't in it?

Sitting beside a campfire, he often reflected on the past. He'd been traveling for months after Momma died, trying to find himself. He now yearned to inherit his mother's ranch, but not in the wake of a terrible fate. He hadn't been ready for that, hadn't been ready to say goodbye.

Matilda Covington was a sweet woman, but a tough old bird to boot. Ol' Blake and Cort were true cowboys and tough as rail pins, but Matilda had a whip-sharp mouth on her and could make those men cry if she so desired. She kept them in line and they were happy for the steady work. As long as everybody respected one another, the Covington Ranch was a well-oiled machine and ran like clockwork. That's exactly why Blue felt confident leaving Cort and Blake in charge when he left for the great un-known.

Blue sighed and shifted some ashes around with a stick. The wind had settled some, indicating it was gonna be cold again tonight. He'd have to bundle up good as not to catch his death, as his mother used to say. She'd always been there for Blue, to tend to him when he was sick, to listen when he had questions. He didn't know for sure, but wondered if she'd chosen to keep Blake and Cort working the ranch on purpose, not only because they were good hands, but good men to have around her fatherless son.

He was still at least a week and a half from town. If what he'd heard was true, he'd have a hell of a welcoming party when he got there. He'd be surprised to find the ranch still standing.

He'd been wandering around finding refugees and earning bounties, trying to find himself, and here he was going right back where he came from. When he left the ranch he was confused, ornery, eager to make his own way in the world. Collecting bounties had come easy to him. At first. Maybe he'd been lucky, the first few having come along the trail that ran alongside his momma's ranch. He soon found that some men were more ruthless than others. Once he killed his first, everything changed. The first man he killed for bounty was wanted for murdering another man's children in a senseless act of revenge. Blue shot him for a family in mourning, and yet he felt a great sense of loss having taken a man's life. That sorrow haunted him with each deadly shot for each sorry bastard he tracked down, only replaced with cash when the stinking body was delivered.

Those ghosts followed Blue across the desolate lands, swirling in the smoke from so many lonely fires. Whispering to him as he laid his head down to sleep on the cold desert floor.

Blue couldn't say for sure that he'd found what he was looking for, but all the same he couldn't say that he hadn't. The ranch called to him. It had since the day he rode away. It was his life. All he ever knew. The bounty hunter shit was merely a supplement to he and his mother's income. It wasn't even necessary. They'd lived well off the ranch, but the way people rode down the path that snaked right beside their land on the way to La Plateau, how could he not take advantage and turn in a wanted man from time to time?

Blue shook his head, took a sip from his whiskey bottle, spit a squirt of the substance between his front teeth into the fire to see flames rise. He'd worried that the bounty hunting would catch up with him. He'd done a few things that were less than admirable in the recent past, in the wake of his mother's death. Taking men in dead when he could have easily delivered the bounty alive had weighed heavily on him. Was that his decision, to take a man's life like that? Was he getting mean? He'd become a bit resentful of life itself, which in turn caused him to become reckless. But destiny called him home, and he knew that he'd have to leave the bounty hunter life in the past. La Plateau was a good place to live. He had a good life there, and he would be perfectly content to retire on the ranch, just like Momma had. With the woman he loved. He thought a lot about the woman he left in Le Plateau. Worried that her feelings for him had vanished or that she'd met someone else. Sometimes Blue felt foolish for leaving her behind. He hadn't been traveling the country looking for a re-placement, nor had he met anyone who was worthy of his love and attention. He couldn't expect her to wait for him either.

He rubbed his eyes, reminding himself that he had to do what he did. It was all a part of his journey. To second guess the choices he made in life would only result in deep sorrow, and there was enough of that to go around. Blue had to stay strong.

Regarding his bottle of whiskey, Blue decided he'd had enough for the night. Last thing he needed was to wake with a head that felt as if his horse had hoofed him in his sleep. He plugged the mouth of the bottle with a cork and slid it into his nearby saddlebag. He hesitated, hand in the bag, and grabbed something from within that he slid out. It was wrapped in cloth. Blue held the object for a moment, his eyes suddenly grave, firelight dancing over their glossy surfaces as he stared at the bundle of fabric.

Carefully unfolding the cloth, Blue did not so much as blink. At the vortex of fabric he was presented with a severed human hand. Black with rot, the fabric stuck to the decayed flesh in spots. The death smell the hand had only weeks ago was faint, unless, of course, Blue was becoming used to it. He didn't bring the hand out all that often, but some nights he had to.

He stared at it for another several minutes, thinking about those carefree moments as a child, only fleeting, like punctuation in a life of manual labor. He thought about Momma and what he would have liked to say to her had he the chance before she died. He thought about how cold his life had become out on his lonesome, killing men who rode the owlhoot trail for what was essentially blood money.

He kissed the hand and wrapped it back in its cloth cocoon, like a mummy's appendage, and returned it to his saddlebag.

CHAPTER SIX

THREE TO A CELL

SHERIFF DAVIS COMBED HIS hair and straightened his collar, ready for a day that might go down in local history. He loathed days like this. Being sheriff didn't come easy. The job was stressful and frightening at times. As many people applauded law and order, there were those who sneered at Sheriff Davis when he walked by, as if they would prefer anarchy to law. La plateau wasn't a town of outlaws, but was certainly far enough west that plenty of them came through.

A part of Sheriff Davis' job was knowing the people of La Plateau. He knew their faces, and as much as he could, he got to know them personally. When out of towners came through, Sheriff Davis recognized them immediately. He'd watch them. Introduce himself if that seemed like a suitable way to gain their attention. If they seemed like real tough hombres, he'd leave 'em be. Just watch and wait until he was needed. Often the cold-blooded mur-der-for-hire types just passed on through unnoticed by the townspeople. Especially the ones with a bounty on their head. Of course, ol' Blue from the Covington Ranch dealt with a lot of those types. They didn't even manage to get *in*to town before they were apprehended and taken off to whichever town had a price on their head. Sheriff Davis had joked about deputizing Blue, but Blue didn't take so kindly to the joke. He was a tough sucker, that Blue, but on the right side of the law, which Sheriff Davis could respect. Deputy or not, Blue had been a great help. Sheriff Davis felt a certain kinship with the man.

Perhaps if Blue had been there, this harmonizing trio would have been taken care of by now. Sheriff Davis regarded himself one last time in the cloudy mirror on a wall in the living room. Naw, Blue couldn't have done a damn thing to prevent what had happened in town. Blue dealt in bounties. Unless the trio had bounties, they were just as welcome in town as anyone else. Sheriff Davis had looked them up, but couldn't find anything about previous warrants or bounties. Really, he had nothing to go on except for the words of Louise Campbell. He'd never confess to using her psychic abilities to make decisions, and he never had in the past, but this was an extenuating circumstance. And what the town didn't know wouldn't hurt them.

There was a knock on the front door.

"That's strange," Katie, Sheriff Davis' wife, said. "A knock so early. How peculiar." She sat on a lounge chair lazily smoking a cigarette. Ever since their daughter died, she hadn't been the same. Mostly sat around smoking and sulking.

"I'll get it. Probably someone wants me for something."

"Well, can't they wait until you're at the jail? Seems awfully rude to intrude in such a way." She took another drag and blew out the smoke in a cloud that just about engulfed her entire tiny frame.

Sheriff Davis shrugged, pitying his wife. He had his work to block out the demons. All she had were cigarettes and time, the poor dear.

He opened the door to a frantic Mrs. Martha Strummer. "They done did it again, Sheriff, they done did it again! Harold's been cut to ribbons!"

It took a moment for the words to register, and when they did, Sheriff Davis knew that what Louise had told him was gospel truth, and the decision he'd made that morning upon waking was the correct one.

Sheriff Davis knew, but had to ask. "Who did it, Mrs. Strummer?"

"Them traveling singers, that's who. They sung him one of them death songs is what I heard. Well, no one's been in the house, I can assure you that. I'd been nodding off, trying to stay awake all night. I went upstairs to check on Harold and found him—" her voice cracked and she broke down "—all cut up. Like someone took a *blade* to him."

Taking Mrs. Strummer into his arms, Sheriff Davis consoled her as best he could. "I'm terribly sorry for your loss."

She pulled away from him, suddenly angered. "You need to do something about this, Sheriff. People are dying, and those men are on the streets. You need to lock them up or get them out of town." Her brow deepened with disgust. "Harold's death is on your hands, Sheriff, I'll tell you that. I hold you responsible. You should have done taken them in already. Hanged them by their necks!"

"But Mrs. Strummer—"

She turned and walked away, leaving Sheriff Davis standing in his doorway.

"Who was that?" Katie asked, her voice even, emotionless.

Sheriff Davis closed the door. He looked at his wife and narrowed his eyes. Had she not heard the conversation? She used to be quick and witty, sweet and loving. Now, she just sat there smoking and sipping off that bottle of medicine the doctor had given her. The sheriff didn't like her taking the stuff, but she insisted, and she was miserable without it. He wasn't even sure what was in the bottle, though he knew the mix was twenty percent alcohol. She claimed she couldn't sleep if she didn't take a couple pulls from her medicine bottle. Seemed she couldn't wake up without it either. He decided it was a waste trying to talk sense with her.

"It's nothing. I have a busy day ahead of me. I'll be on my way now. Don't drink too much of your medicine, you hear?"

Katie looked down in shame. "You're going to take them in, right?"

Sheriff Davis wrinkled his brow. "Take who in?"

"The singers. The killers."

The sheriff nodded. "Yes."

Katie looked up, her eyes rimmed with tears. "Be careful."

Having not seen emotion like this from his wife since the tragedy last year, Sheriff Davis was taken aback. He nodded. "As always, Katie. As always." He opened the front door again, ready to make his exit, and then stopped. He looked over his shoulder at his wife. "I love you, Katie."

Her lip trembled. "I love you too."

The problem with being a sheriff in a small town like La Plateau was there often wasn't any need for deputies, and certainly not full time. There wasn't enough crime for a larger police force, and certainly not the budget. The job of sheriff wasn't one that was coveted, and therefore there weren't people lined up to take Sheriff Davis' place were he to retire, become ill or injured on the job, or worst case scenario, get killed in the line of duty. There was a stigma attached to being sheriff. Little boys dreamed about it, but then they grew up and lost those dreams when they got a taste for whiskey and women or settled in doing the same work their fathers did.

So, without any deputies, Sheriff Davis had to make a decision to deputize a couple of town folks, and under local law they would have to comply. For the job he chose brothers Hiriam and Wilson Stringer. They were both farm hands out yonder at the Picket Farm. A couple of rough necks who made an honest living all week only to raise hell Friday and Saturday night so they could go to church Sunday, be forgiven, and start the cycle over again next week. They hemmed and hawed, but knew the law and deep down were honored and excited.

"Now, I don't know what to expect," Sheriff Davis said. "They don't seem like mean folks."

"When they're not singing killin' songs, you mean?" Hiriam said.

"Well, yeah, that's just what I mean. If you believe that's what they're doing."

"Well what else are they doing?" Hiriam punctuated his question with a spit of tobacco juice. "That's pretty damn mean and dangerous in my book."

Wilson nodded in agreement, he being the quiet one of the brothers.

"Well, that may be true," the sheriff said, "but what I'm saying is we haven't seen physical violent tendencies out of them. Not yet. Today we're going to make a house call. I don't see any reason the three of us would have trouble rounding them up."

Hiriam shook his head. "We oughtta put a bullet in their heads."

"You know we can't do that. This is a town of laws, and I want to keep it that way." Sheriff Davis inhaled deeply and let it out slow and even. "The trial will be fast, I can assure you boys that. All goes right, they'll be hanging by tomorrow evening. I follow the law to a T, fellas, but I'm also a compassionate man. I understand how punishing these three to the fullest extent of the law is the only thing that's going to keep this town from abandoning itself. People are already starting to leave."

"You got that right," Hiriam said.

With deputy badges pinned on their button up shirts, the trio left the sheriff's station and headed down a few blocks to the hotel where the Bridgeford Trio were staying. The place was sparsely occupied, considering the trio were staying there, but the owners, Grant and May Windfield, wouldn't dare break a contract, and the Bridgeford Trio were contracted rooms for another several days. That, or May and Grant were terrified that, were they to evict the singing killers, there would be death songs sung in their honor.

Sheriff Davis walked into the hotel first, his deputies-for-a-day in tow. May stood at the desk, all of fifty-five years old, though she didn't look a day under seventy. In her hands she held the local newspapers, glasses on bent frames resting on the tip of her nose. She looked up above the glasses and scowled at the sheriff.

"It's about damn time you showed up here."

Sheriff Davis tipped his hat. "Ma'am."

May sneered at him, and then offered grandmotherly smiles to both Hiriam and Wilson, who both tipped their hats and smiled back.

May said, "Second floor. Rooms six, seven, and eight." She paused. "If there's blood, I can clean it."

The sheriff was taken aback. "Blood?"

May shook her head. "Just sayin', I can deal with a little blood. Wouldn't be the first time, certainly not the last."

"We're taking them into custody. They'll spend the night in jail."

She shook her head. "Such a pity. You know, you could turn your head, let these boys here have a crack at 'em. Ain't no one in this town gonna judge you, Sheriff."

Both Hiriam and Wilson grinned, displaying a full set of tobacco stained teeth between the two of them.

Sheriff Davis shook his head. "No Ma'am. They're coming with me. They'll hang for their crimes, I'll have you know that."

May went back to mock-reading the papers. "I hear a few gunshots, even some screaming, I won't bat an eye. You can bet your britches the entire town is watching right now. They've been waiting for this. You can be a hero, you know."

"C'mon, fellas. Let's get this over with."

Walking across the lobby with his new deputies in tow, Sheriff Davis made for the stairs that led to the second floor.

Outside there were a few people on the streets, with their eyes on the hotel. Concerned, accusatory, worried eyes. A couple young men stood atop the building that housed the market, tailor shop, and butcher. Below them there were several townsfolk standing on balconies from private rooms on the floor above the businesses. Indeed they were watching, hoping for a show.

At the door to room six, Sheriff Davis said, "Look, we don't know if they're all in one room right now or separate. Might still be sleeping. They had a late night." He nodded at Hiriam, "You stick with me. Wilson, you stand watch out here, just in case any of them other boys comes out of their rooms. You put a gun on them and holler for us. We're gonna go from one room to the other, real calm like. Since there's three of 'em, we tie their hands behind their backs for the walk to the jail, that way they can't ambush us." Sheriff Davis paused, looking off for a moment. "Like I said, they don't seem like ornery folks, but people get downright rowdy when the law comes by."

Both Hiriam and Wilson pulled their revolvers, gave the sheriff a nod. In that instant Sheriff Davis judged the grimy duo. Never thought they day would come he'd use them for help. Figured they would eventually be the ones going to jail.

Wilson stepped back, taking position between the doors to rooms seven and eight. Sheriff Davis lightly knocked on the door to room six. After a moment of silence, he knocked again, this time turning his head and putting his ear close to the door, listening for movement within.

Hiriam said, "You hear anything?"

Sheriff Davis put a hand up, shushing Hiriam, then nodded. "Yeah, I hear movement."

Hiriam suddenly seemed nervous. "What if he's gettin' a gun?"

The door opened. Sheriff Davis recognized Will, the leader of the trio. His hair was disheveled and his eyes heavy with sleep.

"Well hello there, Sheriff." Will yawned. "What do I owe the honor of your presence first thing in the morning?"

His breath was like liquid death as it hit Sheriff Davis in the face. He held back the urge to choke and said, "Good morning, Will. I'm gonna cut right through the bullshit. I'm placing you under arrest for disrupting the peace."

Will smiled bright. "Again? Boy, this seems to be a reoccurring thing with us. Can't stay nowhere too long before the law wants to put us behind bars or threaten us so we'd leave."

Though his mind had done a flip, Sheriff Davis kept his cool. "Come on out here. We're gonna tie your hands up behind your back, that way there's no funny stuff on the way back to the jail."

Will shook his head. "No need for that, Sheriff. We'll all go willingly. We aren't armed with guns, so no worries that we'll shoot."

Unconcerned with the two revolvers that were pointed at him, Will went to the door to room seven and knocked. He hollered, "Rojo, the sheriff's here. He's taking us in."

He then walked past Wilson, who just stood there with a dumbfounded look on his ugly mug, and knocked on the door to room eight. "Up and at 'em, Joseph. The sheriff's taking us in."

Both Wilson and Hiriam gave the sheriff wary eyes, to which Sheriff Davis gave a curt nod, as if indicating that they hold tight and let things play out.

"Why don't you step over here," Sheriff Davis said.

Will crossed the hall and stood beside the sheriff.

"They wouldn't be preparing for some kind of ambush, right? How should I trust you to honor your word?"

Will smirked. "What have we done here to lose your honor, Sheriff? How have we disrupted the peace?"

"People been dying every night under awful mysterious circumstances ever since you all arrived in town. Has something to do with those death songs you sing at the end of your show. Least that's what everybody in town thinks. Me, I gave you the benefit of the doubt, but I reckon I just can't do that anymore." Sheriff Davis shook his head. "It's too weird. I understand coincidence, but . . ." Sheriff Davis pivoted his head and spit like he was getting a bad taste out of his mouth. He nodded to Wilson and Hiriam. "Let's get the other two, boys."

Both Joseph and Rojo complied without so much as an aggressive word. Rojo made a few wise cracks, smiling his big bright set of chompers as he did so, but all and all they were pleasant enough to deal with. Sheriff Davis felt bad about tying their hands behind their backs, but he also knew the art of deception. He didn't know these men at all. Sure, they were performers at night, but for all he knew they could have been traveling bandits who used music as a guise to lure unsuspecting townsfolk into their confidence, rob them blind one night and ride off never to be seen or heard from again.

The Bridgeford Trio were all put into one cell at the jailhouse. They sat on the bench rubbing their wrists as if the ropes had been tighter and more oppressive than they'd actually been.

"Well, boys," Sheriff Davis said to Hiriam and Wilson. "Wasn't nearly as bad as I thought it could have been, but I sure do appreciate your help. Most folks around here are too yellow to lend the law a hand, but they sure are quick to ask the law for help."

Hiriam chuckled and Wilson stood there as silent and stoic as ever.

Placing his hand out, Sheriff Davis asked for the deputy badges back. "Look, I'd make you full time deputies, but we just don't have a demand for that, and there's no way in hell I could match what you all are making at the ranch. But I assure you, I will call on you boys if ever I need a hand. I hope you'll be there for me."

Wilson nodded. Hiriam said, "Any time, Sheriff."

From the cell, Rojo said, "Maybe you should leave those badges on them for just a little bit longer, Sheriff. I have a feeling this town is going to need them."

Rojo smiled, and then the trio went into a vocal rendition of a tune that was familiar to everyone in the room. It was the swan song tune of every Bridgeford Trio performance, an upbeat tune always accompanied by horrific lyrics. There was a melancholy quality to it when sung in acapella.

"We sing our daily death song, for the sheriff of La Plateau. His head will be severed, his arms dislodged, and his feet freed of their toes."

Sheriff Davis went rigid, his eyes widening in horror. Both Wilson and Hiriam grimaced. Shaking their heads, they looked at each other with solemn relief.

"We sing this death song for Sheriff Davis. Blood will drain from his body true, soaking his linens and night bed through. We sing—"

"That's enough!" Sheriff Davis yelled loud enough to startle the Bridgeford Trio, disrupting their song.

The singers laughed. Will said, "That is enough indeed. And Rojo's right. You might want to let those two hold onto those deputy badges. They're going to need them come the morning light."

Both Wilson and Hiriam couldn't get the badges off their shirts quick enough.

"Glad we could help," Hiriam said, "but we's just so busy out at the ranch. I just don't see how we could pull ourselves away for more of this deputy shit, er, well." He looked up at Sheriff Davis. "What I mean to say is—"

Sheriff Davis shook his head. "I know what you mean to say. Save it. You two are just as yellow as everybody else in this town. Give me the badges and get the hell out of here."

The Bridgeford Trio were quiet most of the day as Sheriff Davis drew up the proper documents to make their execution appear as authentic and warranted as possible. Deep down he knew what he was doing was wrong in the eyes of the law, but he convinced himself that he was acting in the town's best interest. He figured no one would miss the musicians anyway.

And then there was the death song they'd sung for him that morning. As much as Sheriff Davis tried to convince himself that it was all hogwash, he became more and more nervous as the night drew closer. Word spread fast through town that Sheriff Davis would be gone in the morning, which irritated him to no end. He insisted that he would be there, but doubt began to seep in. That's why he worked so hard getting the documents written up. If he were to die in his sleep as the town thought he would, they could legally hang the three musicians, just so long as they deputized someone.

When Sheriff Davis walked into his house later that evening, Katie was waiting for him in the sitting room. Her medicine bottle stood on a little table beside her. She'd taken a substantially large amount of the stuff since Sheriff Davis had left for work that morning.

Katie glared at her husband as he walked in the house. "So first my daughter leaves, and now you're going too. What does that leave me with, Grover? Huh?"

Sheriff Davis sighed. "Don't believe everything you've heard."

"They sung you one of them death songs. That's what I heard. Did I hear wrong?"

After a hesitation, Sheriff Davis shook his head. "They sung me one, bright and early. Been weighing on my mind all day."

Tears welled in Katie's eyes and then spilled down her face, following the tracks of previous tears.

"You're gonna die, Grover."

Sheriff Davis crossed the room to console his wife. He looked her in the eyes. "I'm not going to die."

"Everyone who gets a death song dies. That's the way it works. You're gonna die, I just know it."

He put a hand on her shoulder and she pulled away.

"You should have dealt with them days ago. Everybody's saying it, and it's true. Now what's going to happen? You're gonna wake up dead, just like the others. They're still gonna be there in the jail. They'll sing another death song for . . . someone, anyone."

"The papers are drawn up for their execution. I can get it done as early as tomorrow. Already got Andy out securing the gallows. Been a dog's age since we had a hanging in La Plateau."

"But who's gonna hang 'em? Who's gonna preside over their executions all proper-like?"

Sheriff Davis narrowed his eyes. "Why, me of course."

Katie shook her head. More tears. "You ain't gonna be here tomorrow, Grover. You ain't gonna make it through the night."

"Enough of that talk!"

"But it's true!" her lips trembled and her voice cracked.

Sheriff Davis took his wife into his arms, and this time she let him do so, collapsing into his embrace and bawling into his chest, her voice muffled.

"I don't know what I'm gonna do. Without you I have nothing."

Though Sheriff Davis wanted desperately to console her and tell her that everything was going to be okay, deep down he knew that his time was up. He had thought about that fact all day, trying to find some kind of hope, but in the end he knew his wife was right, and he hated himself for not doing something sooner.

That night they ate a modest meal inside. Sheriff Davis wanted to take Katie out, but after so much medicine that day, she was in no state to face the public. He retrieved a good bottle of whiskey he'd been holding onto. She wouldn't touch the stuff, but he was certain that she'd indulged in more of her medicine when he'd gone to use the outhouse.

Despite his insistence that he would stay awake through the night so whatever it was that had been killing people wouldn't be able to get him, he became too drowsy to keep his eyes open. It wasn't the whiskey that did him in. It was an exhaustion like he'd never experienced before. They fell asleep in one another's arms in bed. They'd shared memories of their life together, their daughter. They would even talk about the future until the inevitable would seep into their minds reminding them that there was no future to speak of.

Katie didn't wake up until sometime after twilight when Sheriff Davis' blood began to cool.

CHAPTER SEVEN

ANOTHER WANTED MAN

THE SUN HAD PEAKED and was beginning to edge off into the western horizon as Blue rode into a town called Wrigley Springs. Sounded peaceful enough, but Blue knew a town's name didn't mean shit. Towns were named, initially at least, when things were still hopeful and merry. The ones that were renamed were usually done so because of tragedy, the new name carrying ominous undertones, like Boot Hill or Death Gulch. Maybe this quaint little place was still in its infantile heydays.

All Blue needed was to refill his canteens and gather some dried beef, but he decided a couple drinks in the town saloon wouldn't hurt anyone. Figured he might get some talk about La Plateau from passing rovers like himself.

The place was called Johnson's Saloon. It was dark and smelled of the spilled beer that lacquered the floor. The din of the place was a low grumble of working men wetting their whistles on lunch break and the dailies who offered small tasks in return for a mug of beer, or better yet, a nip of whiskey. The drunks who couldn't keep it together enough to hold down a job and would likely end up dead out back some night after a bad encounter or choking on their own vomit.

After getting a mug of beer from the barkeep, Blue took a spot in the back where he could see the comings and goings of the entire place. His mind still worked as if he were a bounty hunter. He figured to a certain degree that would be the way he entered saloons for the rest of his life.

One thing he noticed right off was that the conversations tightened up after he walked in, as if the men didn't want him hearing what they were talking about. Blue had been noticing this more and more. His reputation was beginning to precede him, which was another reason he figured his bounty hunting days were over. He'd taken in far too many high profile bounties. For all he knew the outlaws probably had a reward poster with his name and face on it just like the law had for them.

One man kept glancing up at Blue all secret-like, but he was no good at disguising his clear interest in the bounty hunter. Blue, however, possessed the ability to look at someone through his peripherals and process the images in his mind. He would do this with his eyes closed to mere slits, looking down, that way no one could see that he was observing the room. He'd honed this trick over the years, way back before he dabbled in bounty hunting when he would go to the saloon in La Plateau.

He recognized the man as Thomas Henry Franklin. Wanted for cattle rustling, which was a damn awful crime considering a farm's cattle was a farm's livelihood. Word was he put a family out. The kids had to beg, their mother started selling her body, and their father, well, he spent the last of their money at the saloon, got rip roarin' drunk, shot a man he blamed for his misfortunes in life and was laid down in the middle of Main Street with a clean shot to his heart. Shot right in front of his kids by a man they'd just begged money from.

Blue would have loved to take this guy in for his bounty, but he had more pressing matters to attend to.

Blue looked up from his beer and gave a sardonic smile, something he'd never done while bounty hunting. There was a sort of hush that came over the crowd, and it was then that Blue truly realized how feared he was, even by the innocent. Some people looked at Thomas, clearly recognizing that he was a wanted man. Blue looked Thomas square in the eyes, something else he only did when he was about to kill someone or apprehend them. Blue sipped his warm beer, placed the mug on the table with a *thud*.

He gestured to Thomas Henry Franklin. "Why don't you come over here and have a drink with me."

At that, the place went silent. Thomas looked around the room, eyes wary, as if wondering whether anyone else recognized him from any wanted posters that might have been floating around. Everyone knew that Blue didn't request a drink with his bounties. His reputation for killing those with a 'dead or alive' order was strictly dead, never alive.

Thomas Henry Franklin was wanted dead or alive.

Blue, knowing that Thomas was shaking in his boots with the fear that he was about to take a dirt nap, gestured with his hand in a friendly sort of way, encouraging the man to join him.

After a tense moment, Thomas obliged. He strolled on down the dusty, dirty wood floor. Every creak was like a prolonged agony, but Blue had both hands flat on the tabletop showing Thomas that he wasn't going to draw his gun all sudden-like and blow the man's brains out the back of his head. That wouldn't be very courteous to those who sat behind Thomas, not that Blue was one to mind his manners while killing outlaws. There was often a splash zone when he pulled his piece, for he thought a shot to the head far more efficient than one to the heart. He'd once seen a man get shot in the chest and still pull his revolver and shoot back with deadly precision.

"Sit," Blue said. "I'm not here for what you think I am, though I have to assume people are wondering about you since you reacted the way you did."

Thomas took the chair opposite of Blue. He was clean-shaven except for a meticulous moustache that protruded from his face in fine, waxed points. "I didn't do it, you know."

Blue shook his head. "Nobody did it, right? Don't bother me with that shit. Like I said, I didn't come here for what you think."

Thomas snickered. "Well, it's my lucky day then. Didn't see you when I passed through La Plateau. That was a stroke of luck in itself."

"When's last time you passed through La Plateau?"

"On my way here, I reckon. Three, four days ago."

"You didn't do it, but you're still running from the law?"

Thomas gave a weary sort of eye roll, shrugged. "What else am I to do? I really didn't do it, Blue. You don't have to believe me, but I didn't. That damn sheriff has it out for me." Thomas paused, and then said, apologetically, "I was pirooting with his wife."

Blue raised his eyebrows. "Oh, well, you fucked the sheriff's wife. That right there is a death sentence. Why would you do something so damn stupid?"

"Heat of the moment, I reckon."

Blue lowered his voice. "I'm not here for your bounty, so you can relax. But what I would like is to know if there was anything amiss in La Plateau when you passed through."

"I only passed through there a few times in the past, but I can tell it ain't what it used to be. Less people. Place had a strange feeling to it. Like everyone was on edge." Thomas eyed Blue warily. "Talk of musicians needing hanging or some such. I couldn't stand to be there for too long."

Blue asked, "How about Covington Ranch?"

"Your momma's place?"

"My momma's dead. It's my place now."

"Well, I heard about that passage where you'd watch for people who got their faces on them wanted posters. I steered right clear of that passage."

"Can't blame you."

There was a silence between the men as they sipped their beers. The atmosphere in the saloon had returned to normal. Blue noticed the barkeep flipping through a stack of wanted posters.

Like an afterthought, or something to fill the void between them, Thomas said, "I got my palm read."

Blue shifted and narrowed his eyes.

Thomas nodded. "I know, I know. It's stupid to believe in that stuff, but I just had to see if I could get some kind of insight on my future. This running around always worrying I'm gonna end up face to face with someone like you is really wearing me down."

"What did Louise say?"

Thomas raised his eyebrows. "Louise? You know her?"

Blue hesitated. "It's a small town. Everyone knows everyone."

"Indeed. She didn't have anything good to say. I didn't tell her about my warrant, and I figured she didn't know about it. She kind of looked scared, as if she saw something she didn't want to see. She looked me in the eyes and told me I was gonna die an innocent man." Thomas shook his head. "Can you believe that?"

Blue averted his eyes from Thomas to the barkeep, who had a single wanted poster in his hand, examining it thoroughly. The barkeep looked up, caught eyes with Blue, then quickly looked down again, shuffling the wanted posters in a pile.

"Louise is a good woman," Blue said. "She's gifted."

Blue could see from the corner of his eye that the barkeep was stealing glances.

"Today was supposed to be that day."

Thomas wrinkled his brow. "That day?"

"The day you die an innocent man. Thing is, I can fix that. For today at least."

Thomas shrank in fear. "What are you gonna do?"

"You're coming with me. The barkeep knows you're a wanted man. He's likely got someone who would take you in and split the spoils, that is if I don't take you in myself."

"How do you know?"

"Trust me. I know. Louise ain't the only one with a reputation. I was coming here for you and you'd already be dead. You're coming with me." Blue lowered his voice. "This isn't a bounty, but we have to make it look that way. I don't kill innocent people, so there will be no gunfire. Just keep your mouth shut. Do it for your own sake. And remember, you should be dead right now."

After draining the last of his beer, Blue stood and gestured for Thomas to do the same. Thomas hesitated. Blue narrowed his eyes to cold slits, gave a slight nod. Thomas stood.

"I don't always give a man a choice," Blue said. "You can let me tie your hands behind your back and we can see how good you are at balancing on a horse without holding the reins, or I can shoot you dead right here right now. It's your choice."

Though Blue hadn't been particularly loud in his delivery, nearly the entire saloon was watching. Shootings in towns accustomed to violence were frightening to behold, and yet people were excited to see some action, especially at the hands of someone as infamous as Blue.

It took all of Thomas' will to turn around and surrender to Blue. If it was a setup, he would be turned in for the bounty, but at least he would be alive. He couldn't be sure what Blue's intentions were. From what he'd heard, this showing of mercy was rare.

With Thomas' hands behind his back, Blue pulled a length of rope from a leather satchel that hung from the right side of his belt. He wrapped the rope around Thomas' wrists, careful not to bind them too tightly. Blue whispered in Thomas' ear.

"You could pull your hands free easily, but only if something goes sideways." Louder, Blue said, "C'mon."

Most of the people in the saloon hadn't seen Blue at work, not unless they happened to be in some other town when he'd captured a bounty. They cleared out of his way as he passed, frightened, inquisitive, expecting more. The barkeep appeared skeptical, watching as he wiped a glass clean with a dirty rag.

Blue paused as he passed the bar, looked the barkeep in the eye. It was a hard stare. Blue reached into a pocket and produced a few coins, slapped them on the warped and stained bar top. Didn't say a word.

Once out of the swinging door, voices erupted from within, inaudible to both Blue and Thomas.

"Just keep your hands in place until we get out of town," Blue said as they approached the hitching post.

Thomas nodded. "That one's mine. Second from the end."

Blue nodded. "I'll help you up. Think you can balance?"

"On my own horse, yes."

"Good. Once we're out of town limits, I'll take off the bindings."

"You sure?" Thomas eyed Blue warily. "How do I know you're not just going to shoot me and be done with it?"

Blue shook his head. "Don't be a fool. I was going to shoot you, I'd have done it already. Looks suspicious as hell that I don't. But like I said, I don't kill innocent people."

Thomas smirked. Under his breath he said, "Not what I heard."

Blue turned and narrowed his eyes. "What was that?"

Thomas shook his head. "Nothing."

After assisting Thomas on his steed, Blue was pulling rope from the hitch when something in a storefront caught his eye. He dropped the rope and walked up the dirt road to the rack of goods that was outside of a shop with a sign that said "Millie's Mercantile".

"Where are you going?" Thomas asked.

"I'll be just a moment." Blue looked back and smirked. "You aren't going anywhere."

At the display flanking the storefront, Blue picked up and examined a beautiful pair of women's gloves. Dainty, white-laced and soft. They were perfect.

A woman came out of the store. "Hello, I'm Millie. May I help you with something?"

Blue looked up. A hard faced man with eyes that had seen true devastation, who had wrought vengeance at the barrel of a gun, holding delicate silken gloves fit for a lady's hands.

"I want these. How much are they?"

CHAPTER EIGHT

NEW SHERIFF IN TOWN?

IT WAS THE SCREAM heard 'round La Plateau.

Despite others having been found dead in curious ways over the past week since the musicians had been in town, no one had screamed upon finding the bodies quite like Katie when she woke up soaked in her husband's blood.

She couldn't get off of their feather mattress quick enough, and seemed to become tangled in the sticky red sheets, fumbling the pieces of her husband that were laying loose from his dismembered body like the pieces of a seamstress' mannequin. By the time Katie removed herself from the bed of horrors, one of Sheriff Davis' arms and several toes had fallen to the hardwood. His torso remained tangled in the crimson sheets that clung to it like papier-mâché. His head lay there cocked to an angle, looking at Katie as if in some way blaming her for the mutilation. His eyelids had been cut away, causing him to forever stare.

She screamed and screamed. Her hair a tangle of coagulating blood. Her sleeping clothes plastered to her body, cool and slick. She refused to stop screaming until someone broke down the front door, and even then she resisted. A couple of concerned residents found the scene, and someone had to pull her away from her mutilated husband. Katie wasn't even sure who it was that separated them, her eyes locked on the last time she would ever see her Grover. Or rather, what was left of him.

It was later, after Katie had been put under medical watch, that Hiriam and Wilson reported having been present at the jail when the musicians sung Sheriff Davis one of their infamous songs.

"We was deputized," Hiriam said. "We helped Sheriff Davis apprehend them musicians."

Frenchy Hill nodded, regarding Hiriam closely. He'd been a resident of La Plateau damn near all his life. When he took over the Mid Town Saloon from the man who'd built it, he became a prominent fixture, having been the ear so many people depended on to listen to their problems, the shoulder so many people leaned on. He was always there. He was dependable. Frenchy said to the gathering crowd, "We need a new sheriff. Any volunteers?"

The people of La Plateau grumbled and murmured, but no one made an offer or a suggestion at who would be worthy of taking on the position of sheriff. No one wanted that death sentence hanging over them.

Frenchy eyed the crowd with scrutiny, though he could certainly understand why no one volunteered. "Anyone?" He jerked his head around looking for anyone who even showed interest, and then he said, "We don't have time to trifle, so I am declaring Hiriam Walsh our new sheriff, on account that he and his brother had been deputized only yesterday."

Hiriam's mouth dropped. "What in the fiery pits of Hell are you talkin' about! I ain't no sheriff."

Frenchy looked Hiriam square in the eyes. "Now you are." Frenchy was a fairly jovial individual, which was one reason people enjoyed not only his saloon, but his company. Now, he dropped any joviality from his voice. "You as sheriff do what you think is right, and I guarantee the entire town is behind you in your decision. I'll help anyway I can. In fact, you just make the proclamation and we can have three men out to set up the gallows in no time flat. I'm sure more than three would volunteer for that."

"But not for sheriff, huh?"

Frenchy shook his head. "Sorry, old hoss, but that's the way the bread breaks. If it were someone else Sheriff Davis had deputized, they'd be the one in your shoes." Frenchy leaned in close enough that Hiriam could smell the rot on his teeth. "You just make a public statement sentencing them three to death and we'll take care of it. Take 'em right out to the gallows tonight before they can sing another song. That's what you do. Once they're hanged, well, things ought to go back to normal around here. Maybe even some of the folks who left will come back."

Hiriam had a look on his face like he'd eaten bad meat. "Why didn't you just make yourself the sheriff if you know what to do?"

Frenchy smiled. "I'm a bartender, not a sheriff. My place is the heart and soul of town. I couldn't deprive the residents of their drink. We get them hanged and we'll send a telegram to the state capitol looking for a new sheriff. They'll send someone along. Then you can bequeath your position, go back to the ranch." Frenchy leaned in again. This time Hiriam reared his head as not to get a noseful of gum diseased breath. "I don't exactly like the idea of you being sheriff anymore than you do, but we're in a real pickle here."

Frenchy walked away from Hiriam who stood there amongst the dispersing crowd. Some people lingered and asked what he was going to do. Others made suggestions. Finally he said, "We're gonna hang 'em." The crowd that had been walking away stopped and turned. Hiriam said, louder this time, "We're gonna hang the sons a bitches!"

The crowd cheered. Frenchy nodded and winked at Hiriam.

After a fine stew made from freshly butchered Covington angus and vegetables salvaged from an untended garden out back, Minnie and her pair of loyal goons retired to a sitting room on the ranch compound to sip whiskey and digest.

Looking through a window, Edwin used his telescope to keep an eye out for Blue, only he spotted something unusual as several men prepared the gallows at a designated area outside of town.

"They've set up three nooses," Edwin said.

James sat in a chair smoking a pipe, a book open in his lap. Turned out the Covington Ranch had a decent library. Blue must have been collecting tomes during his travels.

"There's three of us," James said.

"They don't know we're here. And if they do, they sure as hell haven't made a stink about it. Them's not for us."

"How do you know?" There was an edge of concern in James' voice.

Edwin lowered the telescope. "Because whoever they're planning on hanging is already in jail. They don't prepare gallows for people they ain't even caught yet, you dumb idiot."

"Now boys," Minnie said. "There's no need to bicker with one another. No, those nooses are not for us. With any hope, they're for someone ol' Blue is bringing into town. A bounty."

James shifted in his chair uneasily. "There's bound to be talk. One of the ranchers got away. Surely he's told someone about us."

"They'd have already come for us," Minnie said. "He might be talking, but they aren't believing him. That or they have some other more serious problems to deal with in town. Could be the reason for three nooses."

Edwin, finished with the telescope, put it aside. "No sign of Blue at all."

Minnie nodded. "Any time now. I'm sure word has gotten back to him. He'll do anything to save his momma's ranch, that I'm sure of. And he isn't going to come through the pass like my daddy did." Minnie clenched her teeth, seething for Blue's blood.

That evening at sunset, the Bridgeford Trio stood together at the gallows, nooses hanging limp around their necks. The gallows was a stage raised only a few feet off the ground. Unlike in larger cities with grander budgets, this gallows was not fashioned with dropping floors. The noose ropes ran through a pulley at the top of the mech-

anism with a rope that extended behind the stage, where
two men held each length. Executions in La Plateau were
a group effort, and generally speaking the men who pulled
the rope had traditionally been drawn at random, however
on this unique occasion men were falling over themselves
for a chance at that particular task.

Hiriam stood by, wavering with intoxication. Having
been declared sheriff of La Plateau was the last thing he'd
wanted. He felt as if the weight of the world was on his
shoulders. His sheriff's star was pinned crookedly on his
shirt, a filthy button-down that was the cleanest he could
procure. His brother stood by for moral support, but de-
clined to be deputized when Hiriam offered.

The remaining townsfolk gathered 'round in what
would prove to be the most well attended hanging in La
Plateau history, or would have, had so many people not
recently died or fled.

Louise stood in the back. Though the thought was
ghastly, she couldn't help but wonder what the hands of
these three men would show her. When someone was going to die, how did that factor into their reading? She only
once had the opportunity to read the palm of someone so
close to certain death, but that was very personal. It was her
mother's hand, on her deathbed. That was the first time
Louise had visions while touching another person's flesh.
She'd kept it to herself until she found out that her grandmother had the same gift. She'd learned so much from her
grandmother in the years after her mother's passing, until
the righteous hanged her and Louise's life changed forever.

"We're gathered here today," Hiriam began. His voice
cracked. He cleared his throat and straightened himself a
bit, but nothing could sober him up enough not to slur

his words. "These men have been convicted of not only terrorizing the town of La Plateau, from which resulted in several deaths, but also black magic. Like the witches in that trial. That one . . . the one in..." He thought for a moment and wavered.

Someone in the crowd said, "In Salem, you drunk jack-ass!"

Hiriam shot a wicked stare in the direction of the voice, but couldn't tell from whom it had come. The crowd softly chuckled.

"Salem, yes," Hiriam said. "These three men have been sentenced to hanging by their necks until they are dead. It's an executive order. Ex, expedited for urgency in..." Hiriam's words trailed off.

"For the sake of God," someone said, "Just hang the bastards and get it over with."

Hiriam raised a hand as if to shush the speaker. He then said, "Any last words?"

The trio glanced silently at one another. There was something disturbing about their demeanor. The tiny curl of a grin that played on all three faces. The self-assuredness they possessed.

Will opened his mouth, and with his words, the others joined in with a harmony all of La Plateau had heard before. "We sing you, woman in red, this death song, for what you've done to us is wrong. You'll hang yourself until you're dead, maggots will make a feast of your head. Your neck will snap, your—"

Will looked directly into the eyes of a woman wearing a red dress and coat. He started the song. Another woman in the crowd screamed, fainting into the arms of those around her.

Hiriam saw this and stood there with his jaw dropped. Pulling himself from his drunken stupor, he yelled to the men holding the ropes, "Pull! Hang 'em! Hang 'em good and high!"

The men hesitated for a moment, then, nodding to one another, they did just that, all gripping the ropes tight and pulling back with force great enough to raise the three death singers off their feet and into the air. The crowd gasped. This was the first time anyone had been executed without a shroud covering their head. The looks on the singers' faces as they suffocated was sheer agony and distress. They choked, spittle dripping from their mouths. Faces grew red, eye bulging, the capillaries busting. Their red faces turned deep purple. Some folks looked away.

The men who had pulled the ropes tied them to iron rings that were affixed to solid stumps from trees felled to construct the gallows many years ago. They then walked around the gallows to join the rest of their townsfolk. People gasped and awed and cringed. Though it was relieving to have these men executed, it was horrifying to watch it happen.

Soon enough the three hanged men stopped moving.

But their eyes continued to watch the people of La Plateau. Back and forth in their heads.

And then, several minutes after the execution, Will smiled and showed his teeth. Everyone reared back in horror. Kids fled. Women fainted.

In a strained voice, Will said, "We'll sing ever' last one of you a death song 'til someone cuts us down."

Chapter Nine

At a Crossroads

"It's not much, but it beats starving to death," Blue said.

Thomas used his teeth to rip a chunk of dried beef and just about broke his jaw chewing it. Finally he said, "What is this? Horse?"

Blue chewed and stared Thomas down, then Thomas smiled, indicating that he was joking. Blue said, "Naw, it's dog."

Thomas stopped chewing, and then Blue smiled.

The campfire flames danced over their faces. Backs ached and they both suffered from saddle-ass, sitting on the ground with their legs open to air out. They'd traveled a ways after getting out of town.

Blue sipped from his canteen. "So tell me," he said, "what's all this about me killing innocent people?"

Thomas looked up, fire dancing in his eyes. He said, "There's some people out looking for you. They're waiting for you in La Plateau. Minnie Granger. That name ring a bell with you, Blue?"

Blue stroked his chin in thought, then nodded. "Yeah. We have history."

"Word is you killed someone dear to her who didn't have it coming."

Sitting there contemplating, watching the fire die down, Blue almost looked sad. "Yeah, well, mistakes are made from time to time. We may be God's creatures, but that don't mean we're perfect. Misunderstandings happen too."

Thomas nodded.

"I know you didn't do it," Blue said.

Looking Blue in the eyes, Thomas was at a loss for words. He absentmindedly rubbed his wrists, as if reminding himself that, were the rumors about Blue correct, he'd be dead by now.

"But that don't mean shit if the law has it out for you. You're a dead man walking."

Thomas slumped. "I don't know what to do."

"Way I see it, you can go your own way. We're far enough from town that you can make your journey. Or you can come with me." Blue shuffled around the glowing sticks with his boot and then tossed a couple more onto the fire. "You go off on your own, every damn town you stop in there's gonna be a fight. That is, until you lose. And believe me, with money on your head you're gonna lose. Sooner than later. You come with me and I'll see that no one in La Plateau gets any funny ideas."

After some hesitation Thomas said, "I don't want to live the life of a fugitive."

Blue nodded. "But, unfortunately, that life chose you. It's a sorry thing to have happened, but you got the shit end of the stick. I don't know what you can do. Maybe start with growing out your beard."

"Why do you want me to come with you? That's an awfully generous offer for a man with your reputation."

"I thought we were done with all that reputation bull-shit. I may be a damn fine bounty hunter, but I ain't no cold blooded killer. I'm not asking because I'm trying to save you from your eminent demise, I'm asking because I don't rightly know what I'm up against and I could use all the help I can get." Blue sighed. "I know my reputation. I also know most men wouldn't lend me a hand as much as spit on me. You come with me, you'd be doing me quite a favor, and I would most certainly reward you for your efforts. A dead man walking could use a place like Covington Ranch to hold up in for a while."

Blue raised his eyebrows, to which Thomas nodded.

"I don't have a choice, do I," Thomas said.

"Sure you have a choice. You can do whatever you want. I'm just making an offer and hoping you'll help me out. This is the kind of deal we both benefit from."

"We stopping in any towns on the way there?" Thomas rubbed his wrists again. "I really don't like being restrained like that."

"The trail passes through another town or two, but we can get around them no problem."

After some silence filled with the crackling of the fire and the bugs off in the surrounding thicket, Thomas reached out his hand. "It's a deal."

Blue smiled and they shook.

The men chatted as the fire died down. Thomas leaned back with his head resting on the softest part of his pack, eyes closed. Blue watched as his breathing became steady and even.

In the faint glow of the dying fire Blue removed the bundle of wrappings from his pack. He unfurled the hand and held it close, rubbing his cheek with the backs of the gnarled fingers. He kissed them gently before returning the hand to its wrappings.

Thomas watched in horror through the faintest slits of his eyelids.

CHAPTER TEN

BLUE'S BACK!

TEN DAYS LATER BLUE and Thomas made it to La Plateau. Along the way they diverted from traveling through the few towns on their path, and on arrival to La Plateau Blue diverted their path once again as not to pass by Covington Ranch, as every other traveler did. During the ten days the men talked and grew fond of one another. Blue felt a great sadness for Thomas, who had been a decent man who made a mistake that resulted in false accusations and a warrant for his arrest and execution. He was truly a man of bad circumstance. Worst yet, Thomas' wife believed the accusations. She was prepared to turn him in. He was too shameful to admit that it was all over an adulterous act. That's when he fled.

During his travels Blue had been through towns built around a coal mine that went dry, or on a floodplain and taken out by severe storms. On entering La Plateau he felt like he'd entered one of those ghost towns. Several shop doors and windows had been boarded up, porches coated in a thin layer of dust indicating that they hadn't been swept in days if not weeks. Hardly anyone walked around. Jim Crocket was a fixture in town, often playing his guitar for anyone who would give him half of their attention.

Now his guitar case leaned against the rocking chair he often sat upon. The door had boards across it.

"I don't like the looks of this place," Thomas said.

Blue shook his head. "Not the La Plateau I left."

"I came through here only a few weeks ago and it wasn't like this."

"They must be running everyone out of town."

"Minnie?"

Blue nodded. "If that's who's got it out for me. I'm sure she's not working alone."

"Blue?" came a voice. "Blue Covington?"

Blue looked over his shoulder to see, standing just outside the saloon entrance, an old familiar face. Blue immediately brightened up.

"Blake!" Blue dismounted and approached the man with his hand out for a hearty shake. "It's so good to see you. I'd feared that something might have happened to you, you know with the ranch takeover and all."

Blake soured. "I'm sorry, Blue. Really I am. Me and Pappy tried to fight them off, but they came in like hell on high water. Me 'n Pappy managed to get out, but we had a new hand who didn't fare so well. Some crazy son of a bitch killed him. Shot him over and over again like nothing I've never seen. Don't take more than a bullet to kill a man. It was like the guy was crazed. Scared the ever loving shit out of me 'n Pappy, so's we just ran. Kept hearing the gunshots as the crazy son of a bitch plugged poor Edward full of lead."

Blue shook his head. "Savage. At least I know what I'll be dealing with."

Blake's eyes went wide. "You're going to get the ranch back? You think you can do it?"

"It's my namesake. I have to. I have to for Momma."

Blake nodded solemnly. "Who's your friend?"

"This is Thomas. We met up a few weeks ago. He's a good man. A man of unfortunate circumstance."

Thomas nodded. "Good to meet you. Blue's had a lot of good things to say about you and Pappy. Sorry to hear about Edward."

They entered the saloon to somewhat of a fanfare. Blue Covington was well known and loved in La Plateau. His family had been some of the original settlers in this area. Over the years, Blue's travels as a bounty hunter became the source of legend. People feared the man as much as they respected and honored him.

After having a few drinks on the house and catching up with several of the locals who were brave enough to stay in a dying town, Blue carried on his conversation with Blake. All evening Blue had been hearing all kinds of strange noise about hanged men who were still alive, singing songs that killed people in their sleep.

"So what's the story about those musicians I keep hearing about?" Blue asked.

Blake grunted. "What everyone's saying is true. It's the damnedest thing. They sing songs. Death songs, they call 'em. Then someone up and dies. Killed the sheriff. Killed all kinds of people. It's not so much an exodus that cleared out town, and not what happened at Covington Ranch. It's them damn musicians we hanged."

Blue sipped his drink. "But if they were hanged, how the hell are they singing songs?"

Blake shook his head gravely. "No one knows. No one will go out to the gallows. They're upset and trying to kill us all, far as I can see."

"I don't understand." Blue's face scrunched up. He shook his head wearily. "They're hanging, but still alive? Is that what you're telling me?"

Blake nodded. "I'm not crazy, Blue. Really I'm not. It's true. Ask anyone."

Just then someone popped into the saloon and said, "They're at it again!"

Everyone rushed to the door and went outside. Blue and Thomas followed.

"Shhhh. Everyone hush down. Shhhhh."

The crowd hushed. Faintly, off in the distance, the sound of three voices drifted through the silent, still night. It was a tune the town was intimately familiar with. They couldn't make out the words, but recognized the melody, for they'd heard it every single night.

"Oh dear," one woman said. "Who's it gonna be this time?"

The crowd shook their heads and murmured. "I don't know," one man said. "I don't know how they choose their next victim."

Blue tapped Thomas on the shoulder and indicated that he follow. They slipped out of the crowd and around to the rear of the saloon.

"I don't know what's going on," Blue said, "but I see no reason hanged men would remain alive singing songs at night and terrorizing an entire town. We're gonna wait until people head home for bed and we're gonna mount up with some lanterns and see what's at the gallows."

Thomas looked like he'd been asked to clean out a rattlesnake den. "What if?" He hesitated, "What if they . . . ?"

"What if they what? Probably the nooses broke or something and they're holed up out there, fooling with the locals. I love this town, Thomas. I can't sit here and allow this to happen. A bunch of ornery musicians don't scare me. Let's get us a room at the hotel. We'll rest for a spell and then we're gonna burn the midnight oil."

Chapter Eleven

Midnight Ride

The saloon finally went dark sometime around midnight. Old Craggy Jones was the last to leave, as always. Old son of a bitch had maybe two teeth left in his face. He drank all day and night until he was singing the cowboy tunes of his youth as he stumbled down dusty Main Street to his shack on the outskirts of town. When Blue heard his voice crackling in the night, he knew that meant the saloon had closed its doors for the evening.

There was tension in the air. Mostly from Thomas. He wasn't used to adventure. Blue, on the other hand, was calm, cool and collected. He'd been thinking about Louise. He hadn't seen her yet. He wondered if she still had feelings for him, or if his life on the road and the countless stories that must have filtered back to La Plateau had left a bad taste in her mouth. Blue was a gentle lover, but his reputation as a killer had begun to sour people's perception of him. The town embraced his return heartily, a hero's return, but what about Louise?

Snapping out of his reverie, Blue said, "It's time."

Thomas swallowed hard. "So, just what are we going to do? I've been thinking and thinking and I can't really understand the point in going out there at night like this."

Blue pitied the man. He offered what he hoped wasn't too condescending a smile. "Scared of the gallows at night? Afraid we're dealing with the ghosts of the hanged men?"

Thomas blinked and said nothing, as if searching for the words or too chicken-shit to admit his fears.

Blue shook his head. "Nothing to be scared of."

"What about the people who were out there whooping and hollering earlier? We heard 'em. They're not dead. People are saying that they're hanging there from the gallows. Hanging there!"

"Well, that's what we're going out there for. The nooses must have broke before their necks did. They've been camped out ever since. We sneak up on them while they're asleep." Blue paused and nodded as if confirming his own thoughts. "There's three of them. Two of us. Not the best odds. They've been out there for who knows how long and they don't even come into town. Sounds like they're yellow but they want something." Blue stood and grabbed his hat. "Now come on, let's go."

Blue and Thomas slinked out of their room and through the hotel unseen. They walked their horses out a ways before mounting up, that way the clomping hooves wouldn't wake anyone. Loaded with several lanterns, kerosene, and, of course, their guns, by the light of a nearly full moon Blue and Thomas set out for the gallows.

The ride was fairly short, but dusty all the same, La Plateau having not seen a lot of rain in many months. As they neared and the gallows loomed in the foreground, they slowed, for it was clear that there indeed were men hanging there, which caught both Blue and Thomas off guard.

Blue made a clicking sound that stopped his horse.
Thomas did the same. They sat there a moment in silence,
the night air warm, carrying with it the stink of death.

"What do you make of that?" Thomas said.

They stood several yards away, staring at the three bodies
that swayed with the breeze, twisting and dangling like old
fruit on a tree. Corpses that had been left for the buzzards.
It was a wonder they hadn't rotted and slipped out of the
nooses to be eaten by carrion feeders and turned to bone. It
was almost as if the buzzards were too frightened to feast.

Blue shook his head. "Something's not right about
this."

"They're dead. Aren't they?"

Blue nodded. "Looks that way to me. But who was
singing that song earlier? Who's been tormenting the
town?"

Slowly they moved forward, hooves taking heavy steps
as they approached the gallows.

"Maybe the marauders are behind the death songs,"
Blue said. "Maybe they've been messing with La Plateau,
waiting for my return."

Thomas shrugged. "Could be."

Blue looked off into the distance, toward Covington
Ranch. He could barely make out the place, but there
it was, gleaming under bright moonlight. Just seeing it
brought back memories. He thought of his mother. His
future.

Close enough to the gallows, they could now see that
the bodies were indeed rotted. The mottled flesh had dried
and sunken in over the faces like wax cast over skull, all
slick and wet looking. The strange thing was how in tact

they were, having been hanging there for weeks, as the townsfolk claimed.

Blue dismounted. Took a look around. "No signs of people camping out here. No fire ring. Nothing."

"So who's been singing songs at night?"

"It's got to be Minnie and whoever she has up there at my ranch. They must be doing it. I don't understand why, but it must be some way to lure me here." Blue sighed. "I don't know. Doesn't make any goddamned sense. Maybe they're just keeping the townspeople away from the ranch by inciting fear."

"Them's three musicians, though, remember. That's what they said. They was hanged because they were killing people."

"And?"

"Well, I don't know. Seems kind of strange that them folks up there taken over your ranch would be singing songs just like these guys did. Isn't that weird?"

Blue studied the hanging men, the way their bodies twisted on the nooses, ever so slightly. He hadn't expected to come out here and find himself even more confused. His gaze was fixated on the man in the middle when the man's crusty eyelids opened and a pair of pale blue eyes, jaundiced and bloodshot, stared back at Blue.

A jolt of adrenaline hit Blue, just about knocking him off his feet. He pulled his gun and pointed it at the man hanging in the middle of the trio, but did not fire.

Thomas just about fell off his horse. He made the sign of the cross over his chest.

The corpse etched out a grin that contorted its death-slick face, the skin like a roasted pig. His teeth were white, flecked with rotted bits of his lips, which were cracked severely, dotted with dried blood.

"So," the corpse said with a voice strained by the noose, "someone finally came out here." The corpse narrowed its eyes. "And I don't recognize you, friend." He swiveled his head, dried neck making a sound like leather, and looked at Thomas. "You either."

"What the hell is going on around here?" Blue shook his head. He almost laughed the situation was so absurd. "And here I thought I damn well seen just about everything. Now a dead man's talking to me."

"Not quite dead," the corpse said. "Allow me to introduce myself. We're the Bridgeford Trio, a traveling musical act. I'm Will." He swatted the corpse to his right. "That's Rojo." Then swatted the corpse to his left. "That's Joseph."

The two other hanged men came to life, coughing and jerking around from their rude awakening. They mumbled out curses as their bodies swung gently, and then quieted when they realized they were in the presence of Blue and Thomas, both of whom were stunned into silence.

Blue looked at Thomas, and for the first time since meeting, Thomas could see something in Blue's eyes that he hadn't seen there before. Fear. It was a terrible thing to behold. He'd seemed infallible, as if nothing could harm him or cause him to retreat. But this, this was something unprecedented.

"What is this?" Blue asked. "Some kind of black magic? Are you all under a spell or something?"

Rojo laughed. "Santeria!"

The three musicians chuckled. Will said, "Well, in a matter of speaking, yes, that's exactly what keeps our gooses from getting cooked. Not that ol' Santeria stuff. Rojo's just messing with you. But we have our ways. We sing songs."

"Songs that kill people is what I heard," Blue said. "That true?"

Will tilted his head awkwardly in the noose. His voice was strained, but came through clear enough. "Why yes, we do sing death songs. We done sung one just this evening, didn't we, boys?"

Joseph and Rojo nodded, as best they could, in agreement.

"Why are you doing it?" Blue asked. "You're killing the people of my town."

Will's eyebrows darted up, revealing more of his googly sick-looking orbs. "So you *are* from around here?"

"Born and raised."

Will's chest heaved as laughter erupted, choked out through the restricted airflow from his neck. Both Joseph and Rojo joined in, laughing and choking on the nooses.

"Well then," Will said once he calmed down. "I guess we'll be singing you a death song, mister. We're singing them every night until all of La Plateau is dead and gone." His voice took on an evil air. "They went and did this to us, so we're getting them back. Simple as that. Now that we've seen you, we can sing you a death song too."

Thomas trembled on his steed. He'd made the sign of the cross on his chest no less that four times, as if that would ward off the evil spirits who hung dead from the gallows yet spoke to Blue as if alive and well.

Blue regarded the three musicians, eyes squinted as deep thought prevailed. "Looks to me like you three are in an awfully compromised position."

The jovial expression on Will's face faded a bit.

"See," Blue continued, "I don't know how you're keeping yourselves alive, but I damn well guarantee that when I come back with wood and tinder and set a nice big fire beneath the three of you, you'll go up like old Charlie Cobb's general store back in '78. There won't be nothin' of you left. No mouth to sing death songs. No bodies. Nothin' but ash. You can't come back from ash."

Suddenly all three musicians appeared graven, their faces slack and drawn. The good humor they had displayed was void in the revelation of their impending doom.

Will mustered his best showman's smile. "Well now, mister, let's not get rash about things."

Blue shook his head. "You're killing innocent people, for God's sake. Who's being rash?"

"Well, we've had our reasons. You try hanging up here on these gallows for weeks on end. My neck hurts like a son of a bitch! We can't just hang around and do nothing."

"Shouldn't be killing innocent people either. How the hell do you think someone is going to let you down if that's what you're doing? The whole damn town is afraid to come out here."

"As they should," Rojo said.

"I can come back with a fire or a knife to cut you down," Blue said. "It's your choice. If you have some kind of magic about you, then maybe you can help me. I'm willing to help you if you're willing to help me. But so help me God I'll kill every last one of you on the turn of the wind you try any kind of double crossing, or you start in with all this death song shit concerning the people of La Plateau. That's done with, you hear me?"

Rojo gulped, glanced at Will. Joseph, quiet as usual, didn't so much as flinch. Will reached a decrepit hand up and made a futile effort at adjusting the noose around his neck.

"It's getting old, hanging around like this," Will said.

Blue nodded. "I can imagine."

"I suppose we could cut out the death songs."

"Oh, don't just suppose it," Blue said. "I come back and cut you all down, we're working together. Under my terms. I don't understand your black magic, but I'm seeing dead men talk, so . . ." Blue shook his head and chuckled. "Well, hell, now I've *truly* seen it all."

Rojo narrowed his eyes. "Why do you trust us?"

Will elbowed Rojo's ribs. "Christ almighty, Red. Don't piss the man off. We're good for our word."

"I don't trust you," Blue said. "But you can help me. As well as I can help you."

"Before we was hanged," Will said, "we were upstanding citizens who traveled from town to town singing our songs. That's all we really want out of life. Yeah, we've made some mistakes, let our anger get the better of us, but, well, we're only human. I give you my word, mister . . . what was your name?"

"Blue. This here's Thomas."

Will slapped his hands together and laughed. "Blue? Well I'll be dipped and fried. You's a Blue, and Rojo here's a Red. What are the odds?"

Blue sighed, growing tired of Will's spokesman persona. An arrogant bastard if ever he saw one. Blue approached the gallows and held out his hand. "So we have a deal? I'll be back with a knife to cut y'all down. It won't be 'til tomorrow night, I'm afraid. It's too late, and I don't want the townspeople to know we're working together. They might turn on me. You understand, I'm sure. All things considered."

Will looked Blue in the eyes, serious as he'd looked since their meeting. He reached out his spindly hand. Blue grabbed the bony offering and shook, reminded of the secret contents of his saddlebag.

Will nodded. "We have a deal, my friend."

Thomas made the sign of the cross again, as if they were making a deal with the Devil.

Blue and Thomas rode off back to La Plateau under the heavy glow of the near-full moon. The Bridgeford Trio watched them go, expectantly awaiting their return the following might.

Edwin pulled the telescope from his eye and grinned wide, as he had been the entire time he watched Blue and his pal at the gallows. What they were doing standing in front of those corpses was anyone's guess, but they were in town, and that's what mattered. That's what Minnie had been waiting for.

He was reluctant to wake her. There was no way of telling how she would react. She was a heavy sleeper and cherished slumber in the same regard she cherished revenge. To wake her would be to start a fight, and there was no reason for that, especially since Blue was back in town.

Edwin sat back with his long knife, sharpening it idly. He always had a hard time sleeping. Sometimes he ate certain herbs just to stay awake and ponder his sick little dreams of murder and mayhem. It soothed him to think about sliding his long knife into someone's guts and watching the steaming innards slip from their bodies. He'd done that a time or two, back before meeting Minnie and joining her on this little adventure in revenge. She'd promised him a stab at Blue. Said that they would catch Blue, and Edwin would have all the time in the world to torture him slowly, methodically. Just thinking about that made him all giddy inside.

He thought of James and went sour. Edwin didn't like James. James was a coward if ever Edwin knew one. Oh what he wouldn't do with his long knife if Minnie would let him. He'd start with his ears, then move onto his tongue. Maybe slice off his fingers one at a time. He'd castrate the fucker, that's for sure. Edwin wasn't completely sure, but suspected that James and Minnie were sexual partners, just as Edwin and Minnie were. He wouldn't confront her about it, but he had his suspicions, and that didn't sit well with him. He'd been complacent with Minnie, and loyal, but he had his limits, and when his limits were hit, Edwin could become quite an unpredictable man. Since teaming up with Minnie he'd shown great restraint, and he could feel his inner urges attempting to take control. It was Minnie who calmed him, who soothed the violent beast within, but if she were doing the same with James, Edwin didn't know if he would be able to handle it.

Someone would have to die.

His long blade yearned for blood, and not that of the Covington Ranch cattle he slaughtered mercilessly every other day or so. Not that killing cattle wasn't fun. It was a blast, but nothing beat the terror in a man's eyes when he knew the knife was going to flay his skin wide open.

With sweet thoughts of flaying man's flesh and spilling man's guts, Edwin retired to bed.

Chapter Twelve

Sight For Sore Eyes

Blue slept well after the meeting with three hanged ghouls at the gallows. He and Thomas chatted for a spell after getting back to the hotel. Thomas was a mess. His faith had been tested that night. He'd kept thinking about Jesus bringing Lazarus back to life four days after dying, and wondering how it was dead men could really speak, hanging from nooses like that. Blue did his best to console Thomas, but the man was a wreck of nerves.

Blue slipped out early before Thomas woke. He gathered some bread and a jug of water, along with a few pieces of dried beef and some dry beans to put on a boil later that night for supper. When he returned, Thomas was awake, just sort of sitting there in a daze.

Blue broke off some bread and handed it to his partner, along with a mug of fresh water. "Eat," Blue said. He handed Thomas a hunk of dried beef.

Thomas idly nibbled the bread. He said, "What are they, Blue?"

"The hanged men?"

Thomas nodded.

Blue shrugged. "I don't rightly know. It's magic, I reckon."

Thomas bit some bread and shook his head. "Magic? I don't believe in magic."

"Well, guess you better start believing. I ain't never seen anything like it, but I've seen a lot on my travels. I've learned to accept things that seem otherwise unacceptable. It's just easier that way. I can't lose sleep over it."

"But have they really been killing people? You know, just with those death songs?"

Blue nodded. "I reckon. But look here, Thomas. I've made deals with many men over the years. Scoundrels. Good men. Frightened men. Murderers. I can read a man's soul through his eyes. I read Will's soul and I know that we can trust them. That doesn't make them good. They're murderers. But I've worked with worse folks, I'll tell you that. Sometimes you have to forgive a man's past if he's the right one to help you in a time of need." Blue shook his head. "Even the recent past."

"They frighten me." Thomas bit his bread and chewed as he sulked.

"You need to stop being so scared, Thomas. I like you, but a man frightened makes mistakes. I need to be able to count on you."

Thomas slumped. "Oh, you can count on me, it's just . . ."

Blue stood. "Look, I have something I have to take care of. It can't wait any longer. You stay here and rest. I'll be back in a few hours."

Thomas nodded, sipped his water.

Outside the air was still crisp, indicating that Fall was upon the town of La Plateau. Maybe there would finally be some rain, but probably not for another month. Blue strolled across town and slipped behind the general store.

He found himself in front of Louise's door and hesitated before knocking. He was nervous about her reception of him. It wasn't that they had a bad break when he left, but that his reputation had been sullied in the months since he'd been gone. He worried that she would fear him. Or worse, loathe him for taking up the gun.

Blue knocked. After a moment, the door opened and there she was. Blue felt ashamed that he hadn't come bearing flowers, but he couldn't prevent the smile that spread across his face at the sight of her.

Taken aback, Louise gasped. "Blue."

"I'm back."

She put a gloved hand over her mouth, eyes wide. And then she smiled and reached out to embrace him. Blue took her in his arms and held her tight, a wave of emotion washing over him as he did so.

"Please come in," Louise said. "Oh, it's been so long I've almost forgotten what you look like."

Blue raised his eyebrows. "Oh? You don't keep a picture of me in a locket?"

"I have your picture, Blue, but it isn't the same thing."

"Indeed it isn't. It's very good to see you too, Louise. It's been an awfully long time, hasn't it?"

She nodded. Her face soured a bit.

"What's the matter, dear?" Blue put a hand on one of hers. She made a slight move to pull away, but accepted his gesture of comfort.

"There are a lot of stories."

The look of concern in her eyes broke Blue's heart.

"I know, I know." Blue nodded. "I did what I had to do."

"You didn't have to."

Blue remained silent for a spell. Louise's abode smelled as he had remembered, rich with delightful aromas, lavenders and cedar and mahogany, floral and wonderful to his senses. She'd redecorated some, giving her parlor a whimsical vibe, which he supposed was good for her fortune telling business.

"I came back for good," Blue said, choosing his words carefully.

Louise's eyes widened with hope. "Are you serious?"

Blue nodded. "I'm getting the ranch back. I'm gonna follow in Momma's footsteps. That's what I'm meant to do. That's my destiny."

Louise beamed and wrapped her arms around Blue. "That's great to hear. I'd hoped you would come back, but with all the stories I was hearing, I figured you would die out there somewhere in some wild town. I worried about you, you know."

Blue nodded. "I appreciate that, I really do. It was dangerous, but I always managed. I knew I'd come back, it was just a matter of time. I had to find myself, I reckon." His face brightened. "Oh, hey, I got you a little something."

Blue reached into a pocket sewn on the inside of his vest and pulled out a small box wrapped with red ribbon.

"This is for you."

Louise took the box and gently unwrapped the ribbon, allowing it to drop to the floor. She opened it to find an exquisite pair of gloves within. Smiling brightly, she pulled them out and examined the fine, intricate lacework.

"They're beautiful, Blue. They look expensive."

"I saw them in a storefront and thought of you."

"I'll cherish them forever."

"I'm glad you like them." Blue took a breath, and then said, "I need to ask a favor of you. It's really important. You probably know that my ranch has been taken over by a group that wants me dead."

Louise shook her head. "I didn't know they wanted you dead."

Blue nodded. "That's the word around the campfire. Minnie Granger. She's as mean as a rattlesnake in a canvas bag, and she has it out for me, on account of my past. A bounty gone wrong."

"What are you going to do?"

"I have a few ideas, but what I need from you is a palm reading." Blue hesitated, then continued. "I usually feel very confidant about things. That's what makes—made, me a good bounty hunter. No fear. But this situation, well, I feel like I'm in the dark. I just don't know what to expect. I was hoping maybe you could shed some light on things."

Louise licked her lips. A grave look came across her face. "You know I don't like reading your palm, Blue. I don't like reading palms of people I'm close to."

"I know. I know it's a lot to ask of you."

"What if I don't like what I see? I read Pappy's palm a few weeks ago. I was caught up in the moment, figured I could assuage his fears." Shook her head. "I didn't like what I saw."

Blue wanted to ask what she'd seen in Pappy's palm, but knew better. For Louise, to reveal another person's reading was the greatest act of betrayal.

"I'm just looking for some guidance. Some kind of sign that will tell me which direction I need to go. I don't feel like I can just mount up and ride back onto my ranch. I can't take it back like that. They have me outgunned. But maybe you can see something that will help me figure out how I'm supposed to do this."

Louise looked Blue in the eyes, trying desperately to hide her emotions. Her eyes welled, but she wouldn't allow them to flow over. She tried her best not to allow anyone to see her cry. Even Blue.

She nodded, slipped off her gloves, and held out her hands. Blue offered his and their touch was electrifying. He'd only had Louise read his palms twice before, and each time it was exhilarating. Immediately her arms were awash in gooseflesh, the tiny fine hairs sticking straight up as if the air had suddenly been consumed with static electricity. She closed her eyes and her face stretched back as if contorted, strained, like something within was fighting for purchase. Her grip tightened on Blue's hands. She opened her eyes, but they were vacant, unseeing, or perhaps seeing something deeper than the natural plane of existence. Blue watched, stunned into silence. Louise's lips trembled as words formed softly, nonsensical renderings from wherever it was her mind traveled when she read palms. She swirled her thumbs over Blue's palms in a figure eight pattern as she stared off into nothing like a blind woman.

Though Blue had seen this before, it unnerved him to witness Louise like this. She appeared pained, as if what she witnessed had hard edges and trauma, which frightened Blue.

Suddenly Louise leapt back, releasing Blue's hands. Her eyes returned to focus on the real world and she breathed in and out like she'd been running laps around town. Slumped in the chair, Louise took a moment to gather her thoughts and regain her breath.

Blue waited patiently.

Louise stared at Blue for several minutes before saying anything. "There's a reason I don't like doing that with people I hold dear." She took a deep breath and rubbed her hands over her face. She then slipped on the new pair of gloves that Blue had gifted her. "You're surrounded by the dead, Blue. I . . . I don't even know what it means, but . . . all I saw were dead people. But not like I usually see them. Not like that at all. They were surrounding you."

"But what about me? Did you see anything about the ranch?"

"Sometimes I see images that are crystal clear, and other times they're cryptic or make no sense at all. There are no set rules to my gift, Blue. All I saw was you and the dead. And I mean a lot of dead. But they were . . . well, some of them were alive. They didn't talk to me, like the dead will when I read palms. It was different, as if they had words for only you, and I couldn't hear them. I don't know what it means, but I feel like maybe the spirits of the dead will guide you. Maybe that's what it means. Maybe they'll guide you through getting the ranch back." She shook her head. "It's really all so confusing. I'm sorry, Blue. I wish I had something more . . . legible to tell you."

"That's okay. I figured it was worth a try." Blue thought about the hanged men. Dead men talking. "There might be more truth in what you've told me than you think."

"Truth?"

"Well, I don't know. Something I can work with. Reassurance that I'm on the right path. Something like that."

"Granny primarily used her gift to help family." Louise's brow deepened. "Until she trusted the wrong folks with her secret. She was very good at interpreting the visions.

I sometimes wish I could speak with her, just to get her input when things I see make little sense. I don't know how I could have helped, but if I did, I'm grateful."

"You did."

A blankness washed over Blue in that moment as he thought about the other question he had, regarding the item covered in wrappings in his saddlebag. But he couldn't ask that of Louise. Not now. It was too much. She'd think him a ghoul.

"Is there something wrong?" Louise asked.

Blue snapped out of his thoughts. "No, no my dear. Just thinking about what you said. I better get going. I have a lot to prepare. A lot to do. I'll be in touch."

"Will you?"

Blue nodded.

"Are you really staying?"

"I'm not going anywhere."

Louise smiled and they embraced, this time with a kiss.

When Blue arrived back to the hotel he found that Thomas was gone. Crumbs from his bread were left on a saucer resting upon a little table next to the chair Thomas had been sitting in. A half eaten piece of dried beef adorned the plate.

Blue checked the lobby of the hotel. No sign of Thomas. Grant Winfield, owner of the hotel and working the front desk, said that he hadn't seen anyone. He also said that he'd taken an outhouse break not too long ago, that the chili he'd had the night before had caught up with him something fierce.

Blue stepped outside, thinking that the saloon would be the next best place to search for his partner, when he was accosted by a couple of young boys. "Blue! Blue! They rode away with your friend! The took him, right out of the hotel."

Blue reared back. "Whoa, whoa. Slow down there, partners. Who was taken?"

"Your friend. The man you rode into town with. A man rode in and went into the hotel. We saw it all from down here. He took the man, your friend. Beat him a little bit and hogtied him to the back of his horse. Rode away like that. He was screaming and yelling, just dangling behind the horse. They went that way!" The kids pointed off toward Covington Ranch. "We saw it all. He rode off and said 'if Blue wants him alive, he better come get him'."

"Goddamn! How did they find me? How'd they know which room was mine?"

The young boy squinted. "They watch. They've been watching for a long time. My gran tells me that. Says they have a scope or something. It helps them watch us."

Blue patted the kid on the back. "Thanks. I'm glad you were out here to see everything."

I just hope Thomas can hold his own up there, Blue thought, *'cause it's going to be some time before I can get to the ranch.*

CHAPTER THIRTEEN
ANGER RISING

AFTER THE NEWS OF Thomas going missing, Blue was hit with a sucker punch after being informed that Pappy had been found dead in his bed, a victim of last night's death song.

"How do you know it was the death song?" Blue asked.

He sat with Frenchy Hill and Hiriam at a table in the back of the saloon. Hiriam sipped a beer, both Blue and Frenchy sipped sarsaparilla.

"It's kind of the same every time," Frenchy said. "I mean, they don't die the same, but someone always wakes up dead, or rather, doesn't wake up at all. Guess it was Pappy's turn."

"I've known Cort all my life," Blue said. "He was like a father to me."

"He was a good man," Hiriam said, offering his condolences, and then sipped his morning beer.

"They won't be singing anymore death songs," Blue said.

Frenchy raised his eyebrows. "That a fact?"

Blue nodded, sipped his sarsaparilla. "But I tell you that really chaps my hide what they did to ol' Pappy." Blue gritted his teeth. "Those goddamned sons a bitches." He looked Frenchy in the eyes. "You're sure it was a death song did him in? He didn't just die naturally? He was an old man."

Frenchy shook his head. "There was lots of blood. That's the telltale sign, my friend. There's always lots of blood. Those musicians are creative. They're sadistic. They sing the songs full of violence, and that's how the deceased is found. Cut to ribbons, eviscerated, torn to pieces. That's how we know it was them."

Hiriam cleared his throat. "I'll spare you the details, but there's no doubt it was a death song got him. I saw it myself." He shuddered and closed his eyes tight, took another drink. "I just about puked."

Blue clenched his teeth and slammed his hand on the table, startling both Frenchy and Hiriam. "It was the last one, I reckon, but why'd it have to be Cort? He didn't deserve it."

Frenchy shrugged. "I don't reckon no one's deserved it."

Hiriam narrowed his eyes. "Sounds to me like you've got some kind of plan in mind for them musicians. You aren't thinking about going out there, are you?"

The anger that welled within caused Blue to shake. "Yeah, you won't have to worry about them anymore. It's pretty well taken care of at this point. If you don't mind, gentlemen, I'm going to head on back to my room. I've got a lot to think about."

Both Hiriam and Frenchy nodded, watching with solemn eyes as Blue left the saloon.

Hiriam said, "He took that hard, didn't he?"

"Yup," Frenchy nodded. "Ol' Cort meant a lot to him. He lost his momma earlier this year. He's been through a lot."

Hiriam took a drink of beer. "We all have. Never thought I'd be the damn sheriff of La Plateau."

"Don't expect that to last forever. No one likes a sheriff who's drunk by noon."

"Sooner I get this badge off my chest the better, far as I'm concerned. I'm still not so sure those musicians are done with those death songs."

"If Blue says it's taken care of, then it's taken care of. He's an honorable man, that Blue."

"He's a killer too, don't forget that. I've heard the stories."

"Yup. But a killer on the right side of the law. You want another?"

Hiriam nodded. "I better if I want to be drunk by noon."

CHAPTER FOURTEEN

RESURRECTION MOURNING

AFTER TWILIGHT, BLUE MOUNTED up and rode out to the gallows. On arrival he found the trio dangling from their nooses, all giggly and talking to one another in anticipation of sweet release.

"Well hello there, friend!" Will said as Blue pulled his steed to a halt and dismounted.

"You're no friend of mine," Blue said as he pulled his revolver.

Three blasts came from the barrel. One hit Will directly in the head, and the other two right in his cold, black heart.

Rojo and Joseph squirmed, but could go nowhere, considering they were hanging by their necks. All they managed to do was set their bodies a swingin'.

"What did you do that for?" Rojo asked.

"That last death song y'all sung. You sung that for a very dear friend of mine. He died. I hear it was terrible, too. I been stewing in it all day."

Joseph made an attempt at adjusting the rope around his neck. He said, "Allow me to introduce myself." His voice was higher pitched than his two partners. "I'm Joseph. I been with these boys for many a year. I know we done some bad things, and I know Will probably deserved that, but we was true to our word last night. We didn't sing

no death song on this night," he whined. "That one sung
for your friend, that was before we even met. There was
nothing malicious in our intent. We didn't mean to cause
you harm."

"Well, you did."

Will hung motionless. No blood seeped from his
wounds, just chunks of rotten flesh that oozed from the
holes like old corned beef.

"Did I kill him?" Blue asked. "Can you die from a simple
gunshot like that, being dead already and all?"

"We're caught somewhere in between, Azul," Rojo said.
"We have death songs, but we have other songs too. We
also know life songs. That's how we stay alive here on these
nooses. We sing a life song every day. Now, we'll have to
sing a song for Will."

Blue holstered his gun. "Maybe I was too hasty."

"I think maybe you were."

"But like I said last night, I don't want no funny business. I can get you all down, but I'm going to need your
help."

"We are men of our word, Mr. Blue."

Blue nodded and spit on the ground. "I sure hope so.
Now how about you sing that life song and get your fear-
less leader back in shape."

"Well, it's not so simple." A strangled sigh escaped. "Not
now, not at this hour. This is the most vulnerable hour
for us. Will is dead, but we do have a way to get him back.
Something we rarely do."

"What is it?"

"A spell. A song, but not one we have memorized like
the death and life songs we sing."

"Where's this spell?"

"In a book. With our possessions." Rojo sucked air through his clenched throat. "We stashed everything on the outskirts of town, the night before we were arrested. Over in the rock piles by the copse of trees. You know what I'm talking about?"

Blue nodded. "I think so."

"We don't have a lot of time. We need to use the spell before twilight. That's the only way we can save Will. You see, the spells work with the cycle of the sun and the moon. We can sing a life song every day to keep us hanging here, but Will needs more than that now. And singing him the spell he needs after twilight could have," Rojo grimaced, "disastrous consequences."

"This is what we're gonna do. I'm gonna cut the three of you down. We'll put Will up on my horse, and we'll head into town. I have a room at the hotel. I can sneak you in, so long as we get there early enough. I'll head out and grab your little spell book, then we can see about getting Will back on his feet."

"We have to hurry," Rojo said. "We don't have a lot of time."

Blue made quick work of cutting the Bridgeford Trio from the gallows. Rojo and Joseph rubbed their necks with withered hands, stretched their back and legs, stumbling around like newborn foul.

Will dropped like a sack of potatoes. "Give me a hand," Blue said. The three of them grabbed Will's body and hefted it up onto Blue's horse, the way Blue had done with bounties so many times before.

"Do I need to bind your wrists?" Blue asked. "I don't need no double crossing. Things'll get real ugly real fast."

"We are men of honor," Joseph said. "You helped us, and so we owe you."

"Psh. Men of honor my ass. You damn near killed my entire town."

"We made mistakes, that's true. We were acting out of anger and frustration. I do hope you can find it in your heart to forgive us."

After a moment of hesitation Blue said, "Not now, but there's always time. Just don't do anything stupid. I have my eyes on you."

Rojo smiled, causing his mustache to brim. "Fair enough, Azul."

Pausing, Blue scrutinized the Mexican. It wasn't the first time a Mexican had called him Azul. He'd always taken the Spanish version of his name to be patronizing. He'd never harmed anyone over it, he wasn't that kind of guy, but he'd certainly put the fear of God into a man who was brave enough to call him a name, just to be sure it was well known that no one pokes fun at Blue Covington. He let it slide this time.

They made their trek into La Plateau by the fading moonlight. Blue hitched his horse out behind the hotel and snuck both Rojo and Joseph into his room. He then retrieved Will's body, which was quite light considering how dried out his corpse was. Blue left the men in his room, electing not to bind their hands and ankles. If they were going to work together, Blue was going to have to extend some trust. If they breached that trust, well, Blue would have to blow they're faces away so they'd never be able to sing themselves back to life again.

The cluster of rocks where the musicians had stowed their belongings was out back near Louise's abode. The glow of predawn cast an eerie light that could be confused with the minutes just after sundown. Blue walked off to the rocks, looking over his shoulder at Louise's door as if she would suddenly open it. She would be asleep, hopefully dreaming wonderful dreams, though Blue wondered if she was plagued with the things she saw in people's palms. The ethereal world she claimed to visit when in contact with the flesh of another human being. Blue certainly hoped her dreams weren't plagued, but he could see in her eyes that she was haunted. The visions stuck with her.

At the rock cluster, Blue saw what appeared to be a pack tucked within. He reached for it, and then jumped back with a start at the sight of a rattlesnake. Heart thumping in his chest, Blue moved cautiously, maneuvering around the rock cluster as not to be in striking distance of the thing. He watched it closely. It didn't move. Grabbing a twig that had fallen from one of the trees surrounding the rocks, Blue tapped the snake, but it didn't move. He tapped it again.

It was dead.

Blue grinned. "Clever sons a bitches."

Still wary of the thing, Blue used the stick to lift its body and fling it away. He couldn't help but think the snake would suddenly come alive and strike, however ridiculous that was. After grabbing their bags, Blue returned to the hotel just as the sun was fixing to peek over the eastern horizon. He was certain he hadn't been seen.

Inside, Rojo paced back and forth while Joseph sat in a chair beside a little tea table, staring off into nothing as if lost in thought. The crumbs of Thomas' last meal before being apprehended sat untouched on a little saucer.

"Took you long enough," Rojo said.

Blue tossed the dead snake to Rojo, who jumped back at the sight of the thing. "That was a nice touch."

"That was my idea," Rojo said. "We need the book, pronto."

Sifting through the bags, Blue located an old tome, leather bound with ages-old dust caught in the groves. The pages were gilded, the binding exquisite. On the cover was a mystical depiction of musical notes and images such as a sun, a moon, stars, and even a skull.

Blue handed the book to Rojo, who immediately opened it, feverishly searching for the right song spell. "It's in here somewhere." He flipped through pages, going forward and backward.

"Maybe check the glossary?" Blue suggested.

"There's no glossary in a book of spells. Okay, here it is. The Resurrection Song. Joseph, come here."

Joseph joined his partner. Rojo put his finger on the page, underlining the first lines. "It's in B minor."

"B minor?" Joseph reeled back.

"Song spells of this nature are always in a minor key. Okay, on three. One, Two, Three."

Together they sung the words on the page, note for note, as if they'd not only sung these words before, but done so frequently, as if well rehearsed for a nightly performance. The minor notes had an eerie quality that sent a shiver down Blue's spine, and yet there was something inherently beautiful about the melody. The words of resurrection were unlike sermons Blue had heard in the past. There was nothing Christian about the spell. He wondered how black this magic was. Blue hadn't seen a church in years, having lost his faith long ago, but there was something about being in the presence of the dark arts that caused him serious reservation. He hoped to God no one could hear the song from a neighboring room or through the thin glass that served as a window in the room.

Once they were finished, all was silent in the hotel room, everyone staring at Will's lifeless body lying on the floor, arms crossed like he was waiting to be placed in a coffin and buried.

"Did it work?" Blue asked.

Rojo put a hand up to shush Blue, his eyes never wavering from Will. "We sang the life song in the morning before we were hanged. That was enough to survive the rope, so long as we sung it every morning thereafter." Rojo's eyes were trained on Will. "You killed him a second time. He needed a more powerful spell."

A minute later, Will took in a deep, wheezing breath. He choked on the exhale, erupting into a fit of coughing, hacking up thick ropes of bloody phlegm. He opened and closed his eyes wildly, tears saturating his sun dried face. Looking around the room, his surroundings came into focus.

"What the hell happened to me?" Will asked.

"Check your head, amigo," Rojo said.

Will's hand explored his face, his finger probing the hole where jellied brains had seeped out during the ride back to town, now a thick dough-like paste.

"Well, lord almighty," Will said. "I done been shot in the head."

"Sorry about that," Blue said. "I let my anger get the best of me. Doesn't happen very often, but there are extenuating circumstances."

Will offered his showman's smile, which bristled his mustache and showed off his gleaming white teeth. "Don't know what I did, but . . . well, damn, shoot first, ask questions later, huh?"

"Your last death song killed a very dear friend of mine. I'm still not right about it, so don't go joking around. I might plug you again, and this time they won't bring you back with some song spell."

Will shifted his position so that he was sitting up, leaning against the wall. "Well, my apologies for the mishap. Hanging there, we couldn't think of nothing but revenge. We knew no one from town would come for us, so we figured we'd do our best at eliminating the town. Figured someday someone would come upon us and we'd be able to convince them to cut us down. Actually didn't think it would be so soon. And certainly not a native of La Plateau."

Blue's brow deepened. "It was merely an act of circumstance."

Chapter Fifteen

Edwin Goes Full-Split

EDWIN HAD BEEN HAVING trouble sleeping ever since Blue arrived in town. His sleeping patterns were sporadic to begin with, but the excitement and anticipation of slowly torturing Blue while Minnie watched was far too much for Edwin to handle.

The morning after seeing Blue at the gallows, Edwin had told Minnie he could hardly contain himself, which had irritated Minnie to no end. She was beginning to despise Edwin and his boyish ways. He cackled all the time, laughing at insubstantial things. The poor fellow was going mad and he seemed to relish in it.

Minnie *was* excited to hear that Blue was back in town. She'd been waiting a long time for this, holed up with a madman and a calculated fool. She repeatedly asked Edwin if he was sure it was Blue, and Edwin insisted. He saw the man through his telescope, a pricey purchase several months ago from a shop in some town they'd been traveling through on the hunt for Blue Covington. Minnie protested the impulse buy, but Edwin was pervasive. He ended up threatening the shop owner and getting a hefty discount, which was something Minnie could approve of and downright respect.

The decision to kidnap Thomas was entirely Minnie's. None of them had any idea who the guy was, but he'd rode into town with Blue, so they figured the men must have been friends or business partners. They thought of him as a carrot they could dangle for Blue to persuade him to the ranch.

Edwin, on the other hand, looked at Thomas as his plaything.

"Don't go and kill him," Minnie said before retiring to bed. "I know how sadistic you are, Edwin. I also know your nickname and what it stands for. We need him alive."

Edwin's face soured. "But?"

"But what?" Minnie had yawned just then which told Edwin that she had bored of his trifles and was ready for bed.

"Can't I have a little fun with him?"

Minnie snickered. "You really are one sick bastard, aren't you? Yes, carry on, but don't get carried away. We're going to need . . . some tokens to send to that hotel room Blue's holed up in. That might be the very thing to get him over here."

Edwin grinned like someone had told him he inherited a fortune. "Tokens? I can get you tokens."

Minnie reared away, a look of uncertainty on her face as she retired to bed. Edwin was beginning to creep her out. She figured it was good having him on her side, but the idea that he would be up all night tormenting Thomas didn't sit well with her. There was too much margin for error, especially with someone as unhinged as Edwin.

Edwin gathered some instruments and slipped into the room where they were keeping Thomas tied to a bed. The room was on the opposite side of the ranch from the master suite, which meant Edwin could have his fun and no one would hear. Well, no one but James, whose room was nearby, but Edwin didn't give a damn about James. He hoped that someday he'd get the opportunity to use his knives on the sorry sack of shit.

Edwin entered the room to find Thomas asleep, faced up and tied to the bed with a series of ropes. He was snoring peacefully, which irritated the hell out of Edwin. This man shouldn't be allowed any peace.

Standing over Thomas' sleeping form, Edwin examined his body as if it were a hunk of clay. He thought about the places he wanted to cut and sculpt. He thought about tokens. Minnie wanted tokens, and Edwin had just the idea. Something that would please her to no end. Outside of his sadistic inclinations, that's all Edwin wanted in life: to please Minnie Granger. He wanted to please her so much that she'd drop that James idiot, then Edwin and Minnie could ride off into the sunset, partners in crime.

A rough snore caught in Thomas' throat, causing him to gasp for a second. He shifted, but was unable to move much due to his restraints. This very act perturbed Edwin. A flash of anger came over him and he wanted nothing more than to take his long knife and jab it into Thomas' belly. Just eviscerate the asshole right there and be done with it. Clenching his teeth hard enough to taste copper, Edwin took several deep breaths through his nose and calmed. No, he didn't want to gut the man. That wouldn't be fun at all.

What he needed were tokens. And tokens he would get.

First, Edwin used the knife to pop the buttons off of Thomas' shirt, exposing his chest and stomach, causing Thomas to wake with a start.

"Wakee wakee," Edwin said and he pinched the flesh of Thomas' eyebrow and then used the razor sharp blade of his cherished long knife to slice it off in a clean strip of hair.

Thomas screamed. At first his screams were a balm for Edwin's twisted soul, but he quickly grew tired of the frantic panic therein, and so Edwin grabbed a rag and shoved it into Thomas' mouth, stifling him. He was rough, pushing back teeth that were a little loose. Thomas screamed into the balled rag like a hungry baby in the dark.

"With all that screaming you're going to wake Minnie. You don't want to do that. She takes her sleep very seriously."

Thomas' eyes darted around and around, panic seizing him. This Edwin cherished almost as much as the cuts and the blood. Almost. The look of fear in a man's eyes was exquisite.

Edwin found a tray on the bedside table, much like a tea tray, and used it to display his tokens, starting with the eyebrow. Blood ran down Thomas' face, dripping onto the mattress. This was just the beginning.

Edwin didn't know how far he could go before a man died. He'd gone too far in the past, cutting and having fun when suddenly someone stopped breathing. That didn't necessarily stop the fun, but he much preferred to see fear in a man's eyes as he used his long knife. It gave him something close to sexual arousal. An energy that burned from within like the deep blue flames of the hottest fire. It was like a high desert wind caught up in his guts and swirling throughout his body.

Next Edwin severed an ear. The screams were loud even behind the rag crammed into Thomas' mouth. Edwin smiled, the panicked pleas like music to his ears. The wound on the side of Thomas' head bled a lot more than anticipated, soaking into the down mattress, deep red. The coppery odor filled Edwin's senses like an intoxicating perfume. Next he flayed some skin off Thomas' chest. Just a couple pieces that he could work with later. He wasn't entirely sure what he planned on doing with his bounty. He was driven by bloodlust.

Tears cascaded down Thomas' face, mixing with the blood and running over onto the bed in a pink mess. He shook his head left and right, agonized but unable to do anything about it. Edwin stood back at one point and just watched the man suffer. With a smile, he stood there scrutinizing Thomas, stroking his chin as if pondering some great question, then all of the sudden Edwin pulled the rag out of Thomas' mouth and punched him in the teeth.

"Goddamn!" Edwin said, shaking his injured hand. Thomas' teeth had bit into his knuckles. "Didn't think that one through, did I?"

He plucked out the teeth that he'd managed to knock loose and then reinserted the rag, which was now almost completely covered in blood. He placed the teeth on the tea tray and examined the tokens.

Edwin shook his head. "Not enough. Not yet."

A shiver of excitement ran up his back, and he went back to work.

James woke from his slumber at the distant sounds of screaming. He left his room and headed down the hallway to the master suite where he found Minnie in bed, wide-awake.

"Something startle you?" she asked.

"Those screams. Where did they come from?"

"Edwin's playing."

"Playing?"

Minnie nodded. "Don't worry about him. Poor bastard rarely sleeps. Let him have his fun. Thomas matters nothing to me. No friend of Blue is a friend of mine."

"But what's he doing?"

"Oh, James, don't trifle yourself with such thoughts." Minnie shimmied out of the sheets, naked beneath, her breasts illuminated by the moonlight that filtered in through the window. "He's having his fun." She playfully patted the bed with her hand. "Maybe *we* should have some fun."

James stood there looking at her as if he'd never seen a woman's bare breasts before. He exuded nervous tension, as he was apt to do in most any situation, but more so now with the prospect of getting into bed with Minnie Granger.

"Don't be shy, James. I've seen the way you look at me. I know you want me. Why don't you come into bed?"

James looked over his shoulder and down the hallway, toward the wing of the ranch where Edwin was getting out his sadistic jollies. It was as if James were asking for Edwin's approval.

"Don't you worry about him. I'm my own woman. Way I see it, I don't know why I can't share the both of you. There's plenty of Minnie Granger to go around." She crooked her lips up and offered James a seductive grin.

"Now you come here in this bed right now, Mr. James. I've got something I want to show you."

James swallowed hard, and then did as instructed, closing the bedroom door as he entered. He crawled into bed beside the naked form of Minnie Granger, scared and excited all at once. She reached beneath the covers and grabbed James' flaccid penis. He tensed up at the sudden movement, but his body began to respond, which caused the smile on Minnie's face to broaden.

"You just forget about Edwin and that no good friend of Blue. Let Minnie take care of you. You know what I can do with my mouth, but I know other things that'll drive you completely mad, in the best sense of the word."

Gradually James released the tension in his body. Minnie glided her hands over his flesh, stroking him and guiding his hands onto the curves of her body. James had only been with a woman a few times, and always a whore. This was different, and he realized how much the whores treated sex like a business transaction. Minnie was gentle with him and responsive to his touches, which caused his excitement to grow even more. The last time he was with a whore he had trouble getting erect. Her room smelled like a barn, which disturbed James, and worse yet was the way she herself had smelled. It was a musty, almost fishy odor that made him want to puke. She was dirty, unlike the others he'd been with who at the very least used perfumes. On top of that, she laughed at him and called him names.

But now, with Minnie Granger, he felt completely at ease. She moaned as he touched her body, kissed him on the lips—something most whores wouldn't even do—and touched him softly, urged on not by the promise of a payday, but for the sake of love.

James entered Minnie and felt like he was in heaven. She moaned and that made him feel so hard he could explode, something he'd never felt with a whore. He thrust into her repeatedly, hands on her breasts.

She breathed heavily. "Oh yes, James."

Screams from far off rang through the house, agonized screams so opposite of the impassioned grunts and moans from both Minnie and James. The screams were awful, and soon they got into James' head. He tried not to think about them. Tried not to think about Edwin. He was damned if he'd let anything ruin this moment.

Just as James came, the harshest, most agonized scream of pain tore down the hallway, so awful in its anguish that he felt a mix of post coital satisfaction and deep fear for what Edwin was capable of, especially if he were to find James in bed with Minnie like this.

By the time Edwin was finished, the down mattress was completely saturated in blood. Thomas had passed out several times, only to regain consciousness from some new pain Edwin inflicted. Cuts and slices, mostly. He worked all through the night, savoring Thomas' suffering. It was far more satisfying than messing around with livestock. It was the look in Thomas' eyes. The fear that was so palpable Edwin could taste it like the lingering, coppery aroma of blood that permeated his nasal passages.

By the time Minnie woke, Edwin had gone outside and cleaned up with well water, though he left Thomas in his crimson bed, awash in drying blood and many, many wounds, some superficial, and others life threatening, particularly by infection. Without proper medical attention infection would definitely set in. Edwin had lost himself a bit, but he knew Minnie would be pleased with the results. The tokens.

When Minnie emerged from her room, she found Edwin in the sitting room sipping coffee and watching the blossoming horizon from the window that faced La Plateau. Hearing her footsteps, Edwin turned. Minnie yawned, and then regarded Edwin.

"You look absolutely awful," she said. "Did you not sleep again?"

A toothy smile crossed Edwin's face, and he began to chuckle like a madman. Minnie cringed.

"I've been a busy boy," Edwin said.

Minnie nodded. "I bet you have." Her tone hardened. "You didn't kill him, did you?"

Edwin shook his head, then shrugged. "Almost. He's pretty bad off. But I got us tokens. Really good tokens."

Minnie poured herself a cup of coffee. "You been watching out the window long?"

"For a good while."

"See anything interesting? See Blue?"

"No sign of him. But it's still early."

"So what's this token you took from Blue's friend?"

Edwin jumped up out of his seat and crossed the room. From a table he grabbed what appeared to be a random plank of wood. He returned to Minnie and handed her his handiwork. She grabbed the plank of wood cautiously, holding it careful not to dip her fingers in blood. Her face went blank as she looked at the message.

"Jesus almighty," she said under her breath. She seemed frozen in time, her eyes shifting from the wood plank to Edwin and back again.

"You like it?" Edwin asked.

Just then James came out, rubbing the sleep from his eyes. "Morning, all," he said, and then he stopped dead in his tracks at the macabre display withheld in Minnie's hands.

"What the hell is that?" James asked. He fumbled for his bifocals for a better look.

"A token," Edwin said. "This is going to get Blue out here."

"My god!" James reared back. "You didn't have to go that far. Is the poor boy dead?"

"No, he ain't dead. Not yet. He's plenty hurt though."

Minnie just stared at the plank, mouth agape. Then she said, "I don't know whether to be proud of you or sickened by your mad sense of masochism." She shook her head, eyes wide like a bullfrog's. "It's utterly disgusting, and yet . . . I think this will do the trick. This will get Blue here."

"I don't like this one bit," James said shaking his head. He grabbed the coffee pot with shaking hands and poured some in a tin mug.

"You don't have to like it," Minnie said, "but you're gonna have to deliver it."

James dropped the mug, coffee spilling onto the floor. "Me? Why me?"

Minnie looked at the mess on the floor and rolled her eyes. "Edwin might have been seen when he went after Thomas. Me, I'm well known. I'd be recognized immediately. You, on the other hand, are an unassuming man. I don't need you to make a spectacle of yourself, or this . . . this message. I just need it delivered to Blue, personally. He doesn't know you from a hole in the wall. You just tell him it's a message from Minnie. We can even wrap it in cloth, that way no one in town will see it when you walk through. We wouldn't want that."

James shook his head as he bent down to retrieve the mug. "I don't know about this."

"Well I do," Minnie insisted. "We won't have to do anything like this again, I guarantee you that. This is sick enough that Blue will be here by sundown. And then I'll be happy. Don't you want that, James? Don't you want me to be happy?" Minnie pouted her lips.

James stumbled over his words, as he was apt to do when flustered. "Why, of course I want you to be happy, but, it's just . . ."

"You worry too much," Minnie said. "Stop worrying so much about things other than my happiness. If you put your focus on that, it simplifies things."

Edwin sulked. "You're lucky you get to deliver the message. It's my hard work. I wish I could deliver it."

Minnie approached Edwin, and put her hands on his shoulders. "You did good, Edwin. You did very good. I'll always remember this. Especially if it gets Blue up here."

Directing her gaze toward James, she said, "Clean that floor, and then grab some cloth and wrap this up." She thrust the vile plank toward James. "I want you to deliver it as soon as possible. I'm tired of waiting."

James swallowed a lump in his throat. He nodded, hung his head, and went off in search for a bolt of cloth.

CHAPTER SIXTEEN

DELIVERY

BLUE HAD TROUBLE SLEEPING that night. The musicians were laid out on the floor, bundled in blankets and such from their stash of belongings, probably what they used while traveling from town to town when they had a night in the wilderness. They slept well enough. Blue watched them closely. He couldn't actually see the transformation, but the mottled quality of their rotted flesh had been returning to that of healthy human beings. It was astonishing, and a bit unnerving for Blue to witness in real time.

He grabbed their song spell book and began flipping through it as the first rays of morning began to trickle into the eastern windows. The book was old, the leather binding cracked and chipping at the edges. Within was a bounty of songs with titles like "Love Song", "Death Song", "Life Song", "Mourning Song", "Fertility Song", and such. Seemed to be a song for just about everything. Reminded Blue of those snake oil salesmen who travel from town to town to push colorful bottles of water as miracle elixir for just about any ailment a poor sod had.

The spell Blue kept returning to was the one titled "Resurrection Song". That was the one that Joseph and Rojo had sung for Will, and damned if it hadn't worked miracles.

After eyeing the sleeping men, Blue pulled the bandage wrapped hand from his pack. He didn't unfurl it for fear they would wake and see him cradling the severed appendage. He merely held it close to his heart as he read the words to the resurrection song in his mind, over and over again. The feelings of shame for leaving the ranch were stifled when he held the hand. In those moments he was almost comforted, and yet he had so many things he wanted to say. Confessions, apologies, proclamations of love. He could only alleviate such heartache in those desperate moments when he clutched the cloth-wrapped shame and allowed himself a moment of vulnerability.

A pair of tears rolled down Blue's face, bringing him out of the fugue he'd been caught in. He replaced the hand in his pack and wiped his eyes. After another close inspection of the sleeping musicians, Blue grabbed a pencil and used the back of a wanted poster from the many he had in his pack to copy the musical notes and words of the resurrection song.

Will woke first, complaining about muscle aches and such as he rubbed his neck.

"That's no surprise," Blue said, "Considering you've been hanging from a noose for three weeks."

"Guess it could be worse," Will said with a yawn. "Any coffee?"

"I got makings. Help yourself. There's coals in the hearth. Got a pot and some grounds. Make enough for everybody."

Will stood and stretched and then began making a big pot of coffee. He asked, "You got a plan for what you want to do? Not trying to rush things or nothin'—we're right grateful for what you've done for us. Just curious is all."

"Almost. Seems to me it'd be easy to just sing them death songs."

"Them's got your ranch?"

Blue nodded.

"I suppose we can arrange that. We gotta see 'em first. Can't sing a death song for someone we don't know who it is."

"That's the trouble. Seeing them without being seen. I really don't want to put the three of you in any danger, despite the fact that I killed you yesterday."

Will scooped coffee grounds from a bag and chuckled. "I appreciate that sentiment, Blue. We'd assume not get into danger ourselves. But we do own you one."

"I have some business to take care of. Got to meet with an old friend. I trust you all won't up and leave, will you? I know it will be tempting, but also you best understand who you're dealing with."

"Oh, Blue, don't play me the fool. We've traveled from one side of this fine country to the other. All that traveling and we hear things. You, your name, well, it's spoken of in hushed tones in the back of every damn saloon and bucket of blood from the thirteen original colonies clear to Mexico. I know all about you, Blue." Will sniffled quite loudly, his moustache bristling. He smiled comically. "Kind of gives me an odd pride that I've been killed by you."

Blue considered what Will said, and then he gave a subtle nod. "Word gets 'round, I suppose."

"It sure does. We're not as stupid as you might think, Blue. I know you'd find us and kill us were we to up and leave on you. Honestly, with your reputation, I'm not even sure a death song would work on you. You'd probably find a way to kill the damn song before it took hold."

Finding that last statement amusing, Blue smiled and even laughed, which was a rare show of emotion for a man who'd become so hardened. Will grinned back nervously and continued fixing up the morning coffee.

"Well," Blue said, "if you do sing me one of them death songs, you better damn well make sure it works."

"Naw, we wouldn't dream of it. Don't worry about us. We'll stay up here and sip on coffee until you get back."

Blue nodded, slung his pack over his shoulder, and walked out the door.

He only half expected to find the Bridgeford Trio there when he returned.

Slipping out the back door of the hotel, Blue walked behind the buildings that lined Main Street until he came to Louise's door. He stood on her stoop for several minutes thinking about what he wanted to say to her. Blue was not a man of nerves, and certainly not bashful, but Louise meant a lot to him. He didn't want to do or say anything that might jeopardize her feelings for him. His hope was that after he got Minnie and her thugs out of his momma's ranch, he would propose marriage. He and Louise could live on Covington Ranch. He'd hire a few ranch hands. They'd have children. His life of killing for money would soon be forgotten. He was ready for a simple life free of the hole he'd dug in his own heart by killing for money. Free of mistrust and suspicion. Free of the tethers that would surely take him down if he continued on like he'd been doing.

Raising his fist to knock, Blue hesitated. He thought about the hand wrapped in bandages. The folded up paper in his pocket. How was this meeting going to go?

He put his fist up to rap on the door, but it opened before he had a chance. On the other side Louise stared at him like he was an man insane.

"What are you doing standing on my stoop like this?"

"I was about to knock on your door, Louise. How did you know I was out here?"

"Oh come now, Blue." She smiled, eyes shining like polished coins. "I can sense these sorts of things. Especially in someone whose palm I only recently read. I can sense you, Blue. It's like that with everyone I read. At least for a little while. The ethereal fibers linger before being severed. Would you like to come in?"

"Yes I would."

Blue entered her parlor and took a seat on a plush velvet settee that he'd always liked. The smell of dried flowers and herbs always made Blue feel welcome. It was good to be there.

"What do I owe the pleasure?" Louise asked.

"Any excuse to see you is a good enough excuse for me," Blue said. "But I do have something pressing. I . . ." He glanced at his pack that he'd sloughed off on the floor beside the settee. *You can't bring that thing out. She'll think you're crazy. Give it time.*

"Can you read music?" Blue asked.

"Well, that's a peculiar question. I have been known to sing a tune or two, but I'm no professional."

Blue pulled the folded wanted poster from his pocket. "Maybe you can teach me how to sing this song. Note for note." He handed her the paper.

After scrutinizing the scrawled notes and words to the "Resurrection Song" Louise said, "Well now, I can work with this, but tell me, Blue," She narrowed her eyes. "What is this? Resurrection Song?"

"I can't really say where I copied that from. Not that I'm keeping secrets. It's just . . . right now there are some things I can't really get into. I assure you, after everything is back to normal, I'll fill you in on everything. This song, though. This is something personal to me. I just want to be able to sing the notes correctly."

She scanned the paper again, then looked up, eyebrows raised. "You planning on resurrecting the dead? What, like Lazarus or something?"

Blue let out a nervous chuckle. "Something like that."

Louise set the paper on a table and crossed the room to where Blue sat. She took his hands in hers, still sheathed in the gloves Blue bought her. "You know what, Blue? You are one fascinating man. I've known you for many years now. Sometimes I even think I love you. But sometimes I think I don't even know you."

Blue nodded.

"I'm complicated. I know that. But things are going to change."

"I hope so. I'm here now, but I won't be here forever. The palm reading business only does me so good. I have to find other ways to make extra money. I've been thinking about moving to a bigger city, get a place right in the center of town. That's where the real money is. Up east." Louise tilted her head. "I don't want to leave La Plateau, Blue. Even for all the riches a woman like me could earn. This was the place that took me in after a very bad time in my life. It's home."

"You won't need the palm reading money if you live with me on the ranch."

"Are you inviting me to move in with you on Covington Ranch?"

"I might be. I have to get the ranch back, though."

"Well you go ahead and do that, Blue, and we'll see if I've got what it takes to live the ranch life." She let go of his hands and said, "So when do you want to begin?"

"Begin?"

She raised her eyebrows. "Your singing lessons."

Blue glanced at his pack, wishing he could find the gumption to bring out the hand. "We can start right now, I suppose."

"Well, then I better show you some quick vocal exercises. You might be a natural."

After his initial vocal lesson, Blue returned to his hotel room to find a man in the hallway. He leaned something wrapped in colorful paper and ribbon against the door to Blue's room, then knocked and turned to walk off quite hurriedly, only he walked right into Blue Covington.

"What business do you have with my room," Blue said. "I'm not expecting any packages."

James looked as if he were faced with an angry mountain lion. He stood there frozen in place like his general body functions had ceased to comply with the neurons firing off in his brain. He mumbled out a few words, stammered over some other words, and then Blue grabbed him and ushered him into the room, throwing him down to the floor. Blue grabbed the package that was lying in the hallway in front of his door.

The Bridgeford fellas had been sipping coffee and lounging. With a stranger tossed into the room, they came to attention.

James cowered in the corner of the room, hands covering his face as if he were expecting a beat down. He sniveled and whimpered.

"Who's this?" Will asked.

"Not sure," Blue said. "He dropped off this package, but I ain't expecting no package." Blue looked at the cowering form on the floor in the corner of the room. "What do you have to say for yourself, partner?"

James looked up through the defensive coils of his arms. "She just wanted me to deliver that to you. I . . . I don't even know what it is."

"She?"

"Minnie Granger."

"Now that clears things up a bit, doesn't it?"

"Who's Minnie Granger?" Rojo asked.

Blue glanced sidelong at Rojo. "A woman who wants me dead. She's holed up in my momma's ranch." Blue shifted his gaze to James. "You work for her?"

"I guess you could say that. We've been traveling together for some time now."

"Traveling together, huh?"

Will said, "Now I don't want to sound like a man don't know nothin', but you're telling me you got a woman up there in your ranch and you need us to help you?"

"You obviously don't know Minnie Granger," Blue said. "Her reputation's about as sordid and widespread as mine. She has it out for me. And bad. Now, I hadn't found you guys and found out you have these special abilities, I'd have just gone up there to the ranch guns a blazin'. Maybe get me some help, just to have more guns. Hell, that was what Thomas was for." Blue squinted his eyes. "For that matter, where is Thomas? You all have him up there at the ranch?"

James nodded. "The package, I think it's some sort of message, has to do with Thomas. But remember, I had nothing to do with that. That was Edwin's work."

"Edwin?" Will said. "Who's Edwin?"

James scrunched up his face. "He's a madman. They call him Full-Split."

Joseph grumbled. "That ain't a good nickname to have. My pa had a dog went and gone rabid. Damn thing was foaming at the mouth and damn near killed some kids. Had to put it down. Old pa always said the dog went full-split."

"Well, let's see what we got here," Blue said as he pulled a string to release the bow that was tied in red ribbon. He recognized the ribbon. It was his mother's ribbon. The bow crumpled to the ground. Blue then unwrapped the colored paper. The final layer was dotted with blood and stuck to the item within. Blue gingerly pulled it free and dropped it to the floor.

They all looked at the message nailed to a plank of wood in bits of flesh, an eyebrow, a couple of fingers, an ear, and other organic odds and ends to spell out a name in gruesome fleshy detail, and it was quite legible: THOMAS.

James began to quiver.

"Jesus almighty," Will said in but a whisper.

Rojo made the sign of the cross over his chest and said, "Santa Maria."

Joseph said, "Man did that has right to be called Full-Split."

It took a full minute after staring at the grisly tableau before Blue said anything. "This what they did to Thomas?"

James stammered. "Edwin. He does Minnie's dirty work."

"What about you? You seem so scared. What are you doing with this rowdy bunch?"

James swallowed hard. "It just sort of happened. When I first met Minnie, Edwin wasn't in the picture."

Will whistled. "Sounds like someone's got it bad for this Minnie broad."

"I'd lost everything. She sort of picked me up. We traveled together and things were quite lovely, and then Edwin came into the picture. Things changed. Then she found out what you did to her family." James narrowed his eyes at Blue. "That's when all they could talk about or even think about was revenge."

"I didn't kill her family out of spite or anything like that," Blue said. "Doesn't she know that?"

"I like Minnie a lot, or at least I did. I guess you could say I'm smitten with her. But she changed when she heard about her family. Now I feel like I'm stuck in a spider's web. She'll do anything to get to you, Blue. She won't stop fighting until you're dead." James' eyes fell onto the plank in Blue's hands. "That is supposed to get you up to the ranch."

Blue kicked the plank with the tip of his boot. "I don't know Thomas all that well. I feel for the son of a bitch, but I don't have much in the way of feelings for the man." Blue looked down for a moment, then leveled his eyes on James. "Look, you can get away, you know. You don't have to go back. Sounds to me like they have you living in fear."

"I don't have anywhere to go."

"Sure you do."

"Where?"

"Anywhere but back to my ranch." Blue thought for a few seconds, rubbing his chin and looking off into nothing. "I can get you a steed. You take the old trail out on the south side of town, away from Covington Ranch. It loops around and meets the main trail if you steer right at the fork. You take that on a two-day journey and you'll meet up with a little town called Rock Ridge. Nice people there in Rock Ridge. You tell them Blue sent you. They'll fix you up."

James considered the offer. "I don't know if I can do it. It's just—"

"You can do it. Seems to me it's about time you get some independence. Besides, you go back to Covington Ranch and I'll have to kill you. And by the looks of you, that's not going to be very difficult to manage."

"I think you better take the steed," Rojo said.

"If I leave and Minnie finds me, she'll kill me."

Blue made a clicking noise with his mouth. "Don't you worry about that. I don't think Minnie Granger and this Edwin fella will be leaving La Plateau."

Finally James agreed to taking the steed. Blue set him up with a pack and some provisions and he was on his way. What Blue didn't give him was a gun, but he figured the poor bastard couldn't shoot anyway.

"What now?" Will said, looking out the window of their hotel room.

Blue sighed. "Give 'em time to realize James ain't coming back. Let them make the next move. Soon we'll have to get up close and personal. You'll have to be there too, so you can get a good look at them. Then you do your thing. Sling them death songs."

"How do we get up close without them seeing us?"

Blue shrugged. "Not sure, but I'll think of something. Either way, we'll be ready for a battle, in case it comes to that."

CHAPTER SEVENTEEN

BLUE'S MOTHER

THOMAS' ROOM SMELLED HEAVILY of blood and shit. During the torture session the night before, his bowels had evacuated, which had disgusted Edwin enough to just about kill the man.

Minnie followed Edwin into the room to see how dire Thomas' state was. Her face twisted into a rictus of abject horror and disgust. He was perhaps worse off than she'd expected.

"You did all this last night?" she asked, eyeing Edwin with contempt.

Edwin nodded. "Sure did. Couldn't sleep anyway."

"You need to stop chewing on them leaves that keep you up nights. I think maybe they're making you a little bit crazy too. Man does something like this to another man, well," she shook her head, "I don't right know what to say about it. I'll tell you one thing, Edwin, you're a sick bastard."

He laughed, as if what she said was a compliment.

Thomas breathed low and deep. With each breath a wheeze lurched out of his throat, as if the passage for airflow was swollen or caked with blood and mucus. His wounds had crusted over, but were becoming red with infection. Some of the more deep wounds, as well as the missing fingers and ear, had been cauterized. Edwin had done him that favor not out of compassion, but for the thrill or searing the man's flesh. Those areas with burnt flesh were reddening at the edges, just like all of the other wounds. Thomas moaned and groaned from time to time, even came out of his stupor one or twice, making futile attempts at asking why they did this to him, but ultimately he would again pass out, exasperated.

"Where's James?" Minnie asked. "We sent him off hours ago."

"Maybe Blue got him?"

"Then where's Blue? After the little message we sent him I would think he'd be here by now. Do you think James walked out on us?"

"I wouldn't put it past him. He always seemed like a weasel to me. A weak weasel." Edwin grunted. "Seems too scared to walk out, though."

"I agree. I have him wrapped around my finger. He'll do anything I say. I would think he'd be eager to get back here."

"Then Blue must have got him."

Minnie nodded. "Indeed."

They stood in silence for a moment, watching as Thomas heaved and lurched from the pain. Minnie said, "This man didn't mean enough to Blue, not enough to get him here." She shook her head again. "No. We need a better message. We need something that means the world to Blue Covington."

"What means the world to a man like Blue? Does he hold anything dear? Does he even have feelings?"

"This ranch has a family plot, correct?"

Edwin scrunched up his face in thought. "I think so. Out back. Yeah, that's right. There's a couple of graves out back, way off at the edge of the ranch."

"Good. His momma's buried out there. Every boy loves his momma. Go out there and dig her up. She was probably buried with jewelry. We take the jewelry and we send that to Blue. Hell, clip the old hag's finger off, the one with her wedding band. That message should be loud and clear."

"You want me to dig a grave?" Edwin asked. He didn't seem enthused about it.

"Yes, I do. And you're going to do that for me."

Edwin grabbed Minnie's hand and came in close. "Well, I want you to do something for me." He licked his lips like a salivating dog. "I think I might need some motivation. You know, the kind found in a bed."

Minnie gave him a pity smile. "That's cute, Edwin, it really is, but no. I want that grave dug, and I want it dug now." She leaned in close enough for their lips to touch. "You do that for me, and I'll reward you afterward. You can have me as rough as you like. You like it rough, don't you?"

Edwin's breathing escalated. "Oh you know I do."

"Good. That will be your reward. Now, go dig up Blue's momma, and do it fast."

Edwin dug for hours. The dirt was fairly compact, having been no rain for months. He used a pick and shovel. He pretended that each swing of the pick was going into

someone's head—Thomas', James', Blue's. He thought
about how he'd take Minnie afterward. They'd had sex
before. She teased him with it, mostly, but sometimes she'd
let him have her. She wasn't much of a lover, being that
she'd lie there like a dead fish, but Edwin didn't mind.
He'd actually given the poke to a dead girl once. It was
a little weird at first, but he made do. He'd even gouged
one of her eyes out and skull-fucked her. He'd enjoyed that
most of all, but had never found himself in a situation
like that again. It's not like he'd do that to Thomas or
something. He'd fuck a girl's ocular socket, but wouldn't
dare do something like that to a man. That was just plain
out wrong. Edwin had limits, after all.

A few more hours and his shovel hit the coffin lid. It
wasn't buried the six feet as he'd always been told graves
were, and he was thankful for that. He used a shovel to
scoop out the dirt across the length of the coffin before
trying to open the thing. He couldn't get a good grip on
the edges, and wasn't sure whether they had been nailed
down or what. He had no experience with coffins, but this
one seemed to be constructed very well. The dirt had yet to
rot the wood, though it was soft in spots, probably from
the rainy season.

"Aw hell," he said as he lifted the pick above his head
and brought it down on the coffin lid. The pick went in
effortlessly, splintering the wood. Edwin used the flat edge
and pushed it in the hole he made. He then twisted it and
yanked, pulling up a good-sized chink of lid. The smell of
decay drifted upward, into his nose, and he almost puked.
It was so sudden and rancid that Edwin scrambled to crawl
out of the hole.

He took several deep breaths, decided to wrap a hand-kerchief around his face. Wasn't sure it'd do much, but it made him feel better about the situation. He climbed back in the hole and used the pick to remove the lid. As it turned out, it had been nailed in place. Once he figured this out, he used the flat edge of the pick and pried the nailed edges of the coffin lid, eventually liberating it.

Blue's momma was a ghastly sight. Her skin was waxy looking, and the bottom of the coffin was black with pu-rification that had jellied and melted off her body. Her bones were visible through the skin stretched over her face, giving her a ghastly death's head grin. The dress she'd been buried in was saturated in rot, clinging tight to her body.

Edwin had done a lot of bad things in his life. Horrible things. But he'd done them to living people . . . or very recently dead. He'd never seen a corpse like this one, and it frightened him. He knew this would haunt his dreams for years to come, and he resented Minnie for making him dig the old woman up.

Just get the jewelry and bury her. That's all you have to do.

But there were no jewels. No necklaces. No earrings. He looked down to see if there were any rings, and that's when Edwin realized that one of her hands was missing.

CHAPTER EIGHTEEN

A BIG QUESTION

THE AFTERNOON SUN BLASTED La Plateau with merciless rays of heat. Blue wore his hat to keep the sun off his face as he walked to Louise's place. By the time he got there, and it wasn't much of a walk, he'd begun to sweat.

Louise let Blue in, pleased to see him. "How are you today?"

"I'm alright, I reckon. Got a lot on my mind is all."

"I'm sure you do." She gestured for him to take a seat. "Anything you want to talk about?"

Blue sat in a chair in the parlor, Louise taking a seat next to him.

"Maybe," he said.

"So noncommittal with your maybes." She leaned in toward Blue. "I'm here if ever you need an ear."

"I know you are, and I appreciate that, really I do." Blue shook his head. "It's just, there's so much going on, it's hard to focus. I've never had trouble focusing before, not when I was out bounty hunting. I was always calm and cool. That's how you *have* to be, else some son of a bicth'll get the better of you. Calm and cool, I'd get the better of them."

"Maybe it's because you're back in town. There are a lot of memories here. And then there's the ranch."

Blue nodded. "Yeah, that's kind of taking center stage in my mind right now." He quickly changed the subject. "How about one of them music lessons. I'd really like to get those notes down."

Louise looked down, her face tightened up. "I don't think I can do it today, Blue."

"Why? Didn't we have a good lesson yesterday?"

"We did, it's just . . ." She did everything but make eye contact with Blue, which was unusual for Louise, who was a very good communicator. "I strained my voice is all." She offered a smile that was so fake it could have been made out of wax. "I couldn't give you a lesson if I tried."

Blue didn't like her body language, but he had too much on his mind to bring attention to the fact that she was acting so strangely. "Well, there's something else I came over here for. Something I've been wanting to ask you ever since getting back in town. But it's not easy to bring up. It's . . . sensitive."

Her eyes blossomed. "Sensitive? Why, Mr. Blue Covington, I didn't think you had a sensitive nerve in your body."

"I don't want to do anything to jeopardize our relationship, but this can't wait any longer. It's something I've been carrying with me for sometime."

She put a hand on his shoulder. "You can confide in me, Blue. Don't worry about how I'll perceive you. I know you. I know what's in that heart of yours. I know it's not what people say. I don't believe gossip."

Blue opened his pack and pulled out the wad of bandages. He unwrapped the item, hands trembling, nerves jangling in anticipation of Louise's response. The final pieces of bandage clung tight, but were freed easy enough, revealing the severed hand, black and rotten.

Louise's mouth dropped. "Oh my."

"I remember you telling me the story of how you found out you could read palms. Do you remember telling me?"

Louise nodded.

Blue continued, "You said it was on the day your mother died. You were there. You were holding her hand the moment the life drained from her body, and you saw the ever after."

Louise nodded, eyes trained on the hand.

"This is my momma's hand. I . . . I cut it off after she died, after she was buried. I wanted so badly for you to read it, to let me know that she was all right, but I didn't have the nerve. I left town, figuring I'd be back one day and that maybe then I could work up the nerve, and I guess with everything going on, I did."

Louise looked into Blue's eyes. They were glassy like he was fighting back tears. "I've had a lot of strange requests in my time reading palms, but this is a true first, Blue Covington. A true first."

Blue closed his eyes tight and gritted his teeth in frustration. "I'm sorry. I shouldn't have brought this in here. It's morbid, I know. It was uncalled for. I'm—"

"No. No, don't worry about it. I know you're not a madman. It's a little strange." A nervous chuckle. "Well, a lot strange, but I can sort of understand. You cared for your mother very much."

"I wasn't here when she died. That eats me up inside, everyday."

Louise nodded. "What you're seeking is closure."

"Can you help me with that? Would you be willing to read momma's palm?"

They were silent for a while, Louise staring at the hand, and yet staring through it, contemplating this bizarre situation.

"I've only done this the one time," she said. "I read *live* palms, not dead ones. Truthfully, I'm scared."

"I get that. I'm kind of scared myself."

"What is going to happen, or rather what I *think* is going to happen, is something I, quite honestly, never thought I would ever experience again. I'll do it, but on one condition."

"Yes?"

"You're going to be a part of this. I want you to hold mine and your momma's hands. I want you to see what I see. If I'm doing this, we're doing this together."

Blue took a deep breath and let it out slowly. "Okay. I reckon I can handle it."

"Good. Now, I'm gonna take your momma's hand in mine. I will immediately feel . . . what I feel. You'll have to grab both of our hands in yours, and don't let go until I tell you to. Do you understand?"

"I think I can manage that."

"Okay. Go ahead and hand me her hand."

Blue passed off his momma's hand to Louise. She grabbed it and immediately her body tensed. Blue almost panicked, but remembered that all he had to do was grab their hands in his, so that's exactly what he did. The feelings didn't hit him as suddenly as they did Louise. After several moments a cold washed over him, from his head to his toes. He felt chilled, but gripped the hands tight. When his vision began to swim and fade, Blue realized how intense Louise's palm reading trips were. His breathing accelerated. The room grew dark, as if shadows from the corners seeped out and swallowed everything up. The cold worsened.

Blue wanted to say something, but was unable to speak. His teeth began chattering. He held firm the hands of his lover and his momma, and he wasn't sure he could let go if he tried.

That's when the spirits came. They drifted from the depths of darkness like wisps of torn cloth, almost shapeless, drifting around the room as if drawn to it somehow. Blue's heartbeat accelerated as fear swam in the great pool of his unraveling consciousness. He tried to speak, but was still unable to. Louise sat before him, decidedly calmer, though her eyes were wide and listless and her mouth slack.

The spectral beings floated around and around like bugs drawn to a lantern on a hot summer night. Some of them had faces, others seemed to be even more faded, as if their essence were slowly dissolving into nothing.

"Matilda. Covington." Louise's voice was strained and fragile.

As if hearing her name, a figure slowly emerged from the black pit that surrounded Blue and Louise. At the sight of his mother, tears ran down Blue's face. His lips trembled. He wanted badly to speak with her, but he couldn't form words.

Matilda stood before her son, looked into his eyes, and smiled big and bright, just like she used to do when he was a little boy. He loved that smile. He cherished it. He'd thought of it every night of his travels as he cradled her hand in his.

"You weren't there when I died," Matilda said, her voice paper thin, "but don't worry. You have nothing to be ashamed of. You were working hard, making a living. I respect that. I was very well taken care of in my final days. Pappy, Blake, and all the people of La Plateau were very generous."

Blue closed his eyes tight and nodded, tears running down his face. When he opened them he was greeted with a blurry vision of his spectral mother looking upon him lovingly, and though he couldn't speak with her, he could tell that she felt the warmth and love exploding from his heart.

Louise found her voice and said, "Do you have any messages from beyond? Anything to help Blue?"

Matilda's face soured, and she seemed to scrutinize the question. "I bear no messages. I cannot speak of my spiritual presence, for it is forbidden to do so. But I can feel a presence over my body. Not my spiritual body, but my physical body, for there are still fibers of my spirit that cling to the grave." Matilda shuddered, which caused her ethereal being to shiver and shake like a draft had blown through the room. "They've desecrated my earthly tomb. That is all I can say."

Blue cringed. He wanted to ask his mother what that meant. He wanted to tell her that he was going to take over the ranch and follow in her footsteps, that he was finished living dangerously, that he was ready to settle down. He wanted to say so much, but nothing would come out.

Matilda nodded again, as if she heard the thoughts running through Blue's mind and offered her approval. Her form began to slowly fade. Blue made agonized sounds, his face twisting into a mask of sheer emotion, and then he said, "I love you, momma."

Just as Matilda faded into the ethers, she smiled for him again and said, "I Love you too, Baby Blue."

The spectral forms dissipated as well, leaving the room a cloak of darkness. Louise whispered, "You can let go now."

Blue let go of Louise and his momma's hands. The darkness slipped back into the nooks and crannies of the room, bringing a flood of light that almost hurt Blue's eyes. He breathed heavily, his face glossy with tears. Louise gave him time before she spoke.

"I hope it was everything you were expecting," she finally said.

Blue wiped his face in haste, suddenly embarrassed about the tears shed. He looked at Louise like a child who'd just seen a magic trick. "Everything and more."

She nodded, satisfied with her work. "I'm glad you got to see. I've never done that before. I really didn't know it would work."

After a moment, Blue said, "It really was amazing, even though I must confess I was terrified. I couldn't speak."

"Finding your voice in the ethereal realm can be difficult, but I'm glad you did. That was a very special moment."

"Yes, I'm glad I did too. But what about what she said, about her physical body? She said it is being desecrated."

"It's the folks want you dead, up there at your ranch. They must have . . . I know it sounds morbid, but they must have dug up your momma's grave."

Blue cringed. "Why in the hell would they do a thing like that?"

"Same reason they'd sent you a plank of wood with a name written in flesh. They're sick and demented."

"Now they've gone too far." Blue stood and headed for the door. "I think it's high time I pay them a visit."

CHAPTER NINETEEN

A VISIT TO COVINGTON RANCH

THE FIRST THING BLUE said when he returned to the hotel room was, "It's time."

"Time?" Rojo said, eyebrows tilted up comically. "Time for what, Señor Azul?"

Blue squinted his eyes. *Azul?* "We're heading up to Covington Ranch. I want you to get a good look at them. I don't know how many there are, but we'll sneak around and spy on them 'til you guys see them. Then tonight I want death songs."

"Well," Will said with a chuckle. "Thing is we can only do one death song a night, but we'd be more than happy to fire one off tonight. I don't know about you fellas, but I'm ready to take care of this whole business so's we can get back to traveling the planes and singing our songs."

Joseph and Rojo murmured out agreements.

"One a night, huh? So there's rules to them spells in that there book?"

"Damn right there is," Will said. "The biggest rule is that most spells can only be used once in a day. Particularly the more nasty ones. Man gets a spell that kills people in their sleep and he could go crazy with it if there weren't some kind of rules. Now, don't ask me how the rules work. They just do."

"Where in the hell did you folks get that book anyway? You don't seem like the type to be roaming around with a book of black magic."

Will raised his eyebrows and looked over his shoulder to Joseph.

Joseph cleared his throat. "I'm one responsible for the book." His voice oozed out like fresh sap from a tree. "Got it from a strange old lady. She was downright witchy. Kinda scary, really. But we got along well enough. Don't think nobody liked her. Me, I was down on my luck, fixin' to set out on a bad path, maybe try to rob a bank or stick people up on the highway. Lady had a beautiful singing voice, and that's about all I knew to do. I loved singing. We'd sing together. I think she took a fancy to me, but like I said, she was an awful strange woman. I didn't have the same feelings for her.

"She got sick out of nowhere. Bad sick. I was the only one at her bedside. One day she pulls out this here book, gives it to me. Tells me it's full of song spells that will heal or kill, as she put it. Said she was tired of being alive, that the book had served her well for right over two hundred years."

"Two hundred years?" Blue echoed.

"That's what she said. I thought she was delusional, being on her deathbed and all. She died shortly afterward. I've had the book ever since. Through trial and error we found out that there are rules to the spells. They're not meant to be overused, I reckon."

"It's a good thing I'm no Christian," Blue said. "A book like that would surely be the work of the devil, if I believed in such things." Blue grabbed a second gun and put it in the empty holster on the right side of his gun belt. "Do you all have to see their faces for the death song?"

"No, sir," Will said. "So long as one of us sees it, the song will work like a charm, just so long as the man who sees the face is singing. That's the key."

"In that case, you're coming with me, Will. You two stay here. I think it will be easier for us to sneak around as a duo than a quartet. They see us and things are going to get ugly fast."

Will nodded his approval. "Fair enough."

"Here." Blue handed Will a revolver. "You're gonna need this, just in case. My guns have hair triggers, so don't even put your finger on the trigger unless you plan on firing that thing. And don't fire that thing unless you plan on killing."

Will examined the gun and nodded. "You wouldn't happen to have another holster, would you?"

Blue shook his head. "Suppose you'll have to tuck it into your belt. You boys don't have firearms?"

They shook their heads.

Blue's face scrunched up in something like shock and disgust. "So you been traveling around the country you don't got guns? That what you're telling me?"

Joseph patted the song spell book. "Everything we need we got in this here book."

"That's damned impressive. I ain't never known no one travels across this land don't own at least one revolver. You boys have balls."

Rojo laughed. "We might have *cajones grande*, but that book is our salvation."

After loading up on ammo and a quick bite to eat, Blue and Will set off for Covington Ranch. They rode horses to the outskirts of town where they hitched them at a water trough, and then made the rest of their short journey on foot.

"There's a main road goes by the ranch," Blue said. "Travelers pass through there all the time. My guess is they're looking out for us, which means they'll expect us to come in from the north, as if coming directly from town. We're gonna head around the eastern side. There's an area with a copse of trees. We go through there to get closer, then we have to use bushes for cover. We should be able to get close enough you can get a good look. Of course, that all depends on if anybody goes outside. I imagine they will. There's an area on the eastern side of the ranch where there's an underground spring that feeds our well. The trees grow good there. If we can make it to that point, we should have a damn fine vantage."

"I'll follow your lead, Blue."

"Good man. Let's go."

Will followed Blue's direction and they made it to the copse of trees. From that point they could see the eastern edge of the ranch. What they didn't see was Minnie or Edwin or whoever else they had there for backup, if anyone at all. Blue scanned the dusty pasture between them and the underground spring where trees grew thick and close enough together to provide good hiding.

"We're gonna have to make a run for it, aren't we?" Will said.

"I think you're right about that. Bushes are really spread out this year."

"Not very big, either."

"We get over to those trees, we'll be good to take watch for a while. We're gonna have to run back, but we'll cross that bridge later. You fast, Will?"

Will made a face, sucking air through clenched teeth. "I'm right good with a guitar, but I do all my traveling on horse."

Blue nudged Will in the ribs with his elbow. "Try to keep up." And he was off and running.

Will cursed under his breath, taking off after Blue.

Blue looked back at Will and he smiled, which caused Will to pick up the pace and run harder. The hot air almost felt cool rushing over Blue's face. By the time they made it to the shade trees over the underground spring, Will was laughing. Surprisingly enough, Blue was laughing too, desert air filling his lungs as he pulled in deep breaths.

Their laughter was short lived, considering the situation, but it felt damn good, and broke up the monotony of the task at hand.

"Beat you," Blue said.

"Well hell, you barely gave me a fighting chance."

Blue shook his head. "Me and my friends used to race from the those trees to these ones, back when we were little. I don't know, it all just sort of hit me. For a minute there I felt like a kid again."

Will crouched over, hands on his knees. He took in heavy breaths. "I feel like I was just chased by a pack of coyotes. I'm winded."

"You need more running and less guitar, I guess."

"Hell, I don't even have a guitar anymore. Someone destroyed mine just before we was hanged."

"You can't really blame them for that, now can you?"

"It was a fine guitar. They should have just kept it for themselves."

"There's a general store in town, sells all kinds of things. They might have a guitar in there. Probably not like the one you had, but a guitar's a guitar, especially for a traveling musician."

"I'll keep that in mind."

"Let's hunker down and keep watch. This could take a while."

They made themselves as comfortable as possible, doing best to use bush and tree branches to hide their location. They had a great vantage of three quarters of the ranch.

"Doesn't look a whole lot different from when I left," Blue said. "Sides the dead cattle."

"I smell 'em ever once in a while, when the wind is right."

"They look like they've been mutilated."

Will nodded.

Blue said, "I don't know what kind of sick bastard mutilates livestock like that."

"The same kind of sick bastard that writes a man's name in his own damn flesh on a goddamned piece of drift wood, that's who."

"Yup. Edwin Full-Split. I've heard of him, but we've never crossed paths. At least not that I know. He's reputed to be a real sick bastard. He's wanted, far as I know. I never went after him. Rape, murder, highway robbery. If it's against the law, he's done it."

"So he's in there, and this Minnie woman you spoke of is in there. Anyone else that you know of, Blue?"

Blue shook his head. "No."

After a couple of hours sweltering in the shade of the trees, someone finally emerged from the house. The man walked out with his shirt off, wearing a pair of dingy duds that looked like they hadn't been washed, well, ever. His duds were stained with dark splatters of what appeared to be blood. He carried a long knife in one hand. His gait was deliberate.

He headed toward the rear of the property, toward the family plot.

"What's he doing?" Will asked.

"I don't even want to know. Get a good look at him. Don't forget that face."

"Oh, I never forget a face."

Once Edwin was over a small bluff, they couldn't see him any more. The family plot was just over that bluff. Blue hadn't told the musicians about what he'd done at Louise's place. It was too personal. He now wondered if Edwin was the one desecrating his mother's grave. Was that what he was up to right now?

"I bet you could get a good shot off on him," Will said. "Word around the campfire is you're a damn fine shot."

"I am. But that will only start a gunfight, and we're at a disadvantage. We don't know how many people are in there."

"That James guy made it sound like just Minnie and Edwin."

"Might be, but that's a risk I don't want to take. If you can remember this Edwin fella's face, you can sing him a death song. With him gone, that might leave only Minnie. Unless, of course, she shows up outside and you get a good look at her."

Off in the distance came a hacking sound, followed by exasperated grunts, and then a cry of triumph. Faintly the words, "You old bitch!" could be heard.

Eyes clenched tight, Blue did everything he could to calm himself. His hand went to his gun, but he didn't pull it. Just felt it there. He wanted so badly to plug that son of a bitch when he came back over the bluff, but he knew better. To allow his emotions to get the better of him would put both he and Will in danger.

Noticing Blue's hand hovering over the stock of his revolver, Will said, "He's gonna die, Blue. Don't you worry about that. He's gonna die."

Edwin's form came into view. The long knife was still clutched in his right hand, but something else dangled from his left.

"What's he carrying," Blue asked, squinting. "Some kind of satchel?"

As Edwin strutted forth and came into view, Will shook his head. "Don't look, Blue. You don't need to see this."

"What is it?" Blue squinted again, and then it came into view. Edwin carried the severed head of his momma, dangling from a clenched fist by her gray hair. Blue pulled his revolver and pointed.

Will tensed. "Don't do it," he whispered.

Blue followed Edwin with the barrel of the gun until the bastard was out of sight. He then holstered it and let out a breath he'd been holding before he slumped against a tree trunk. "Jesus Christ, Will, the piece of shit's got my momma's head." Tears welled in Blue's eyes. He did nothing to conceal them. "What's he gonna do with her head, Will?"

Will was stunned into silence. He felt for Blue, but didn't know what to say or do to comfort him. "I don't know, Blue. Really I don't. But mark my words, he's gonna suffer."

Blue placed a hand on Will's shoulder. "I never thought I'd want another human being to suffer, not really. My marks were quick. Just a shot. Humane, even for people who were dirty scoundrels." Blue's lips trembled, and a tear slipped down his face. "You make him suffer. Do that for me."

They remained at their post for another couple of hours, idly chewing on dried beef and sipping from a leather water bag. They talked, and as it turned out Blue was beginning to like Will. He still had a hard time forgiving him for what he'd done to Cort and the rest of La Plateau, but Blue was a man who believed in redemption, and as far as he was concerned, Will was well on his way to repentance.

"I don't think Minnie's coming out," Blue said. "Let's get back to town. I need to cool off a bit. I'm hotter than a tin pot in the noonday sun."

They walked from the underground spring to the copse of trees rather than have another race. Just as they got to the copse, a voice called out, "Hey! What the hell are you doing here?"

Blue turned to see Edwin pointing a gun at them. A sick feeling swelled from his stomach. His instinct was to pull a revolver and shoot first, but this wasn't the right moment to engage, and he couldn't be sure that Will would be his best ally in a gunfight.

Looking at Will, Blue raised his eyebrows and said, "Run!"

Blue and Will ran into the copse of trees and didn't look back.

Minnie came up behind Edwin and pushed his arm down. "Don't shoot. That was Blue. I don't want him shot like this. It's too personal. I want to kill him myself."

Edwin pouted like a child. "I thought you said I could have him."

Minnie grimaced. "You can have him after I'm done."

Later that evening Blue and the Bridgeford Trio sat in the glow of candles and oil lamps. It was time for a death song.

"Any suggestions, Blue?" Will asked. "When we sing the death song, we improvise and sing as many verses as we like. We've got the verses written out here." Will tapped a paper with the back of his hand. "What we sing is what happens to the person on the receiving end of the song."

"No. I'll leave it to you. I hate that son of a bitch, but I just don't have it in me to think about things like torturing him. That's just not the way my mind operates."

"No problemo," Will said. "We'll sing the song and give him our nastiest, most depraved thoughts. I want to make sure Edwin *really* goes Full-Split. You don't have to listen if you don't want to. It's going to get . . . vile. I know how he's hurt you, Blue. I want to get him back."

Blue thought on this for moment, candle light dancing across his rugged face. "I'll stay. I won't be able to see what happens to him, so I better hear about it. Don't hold back. I'm not a man of revenge, but I've never hated anyone more than I hate a man who defiles Momma's remains like that."

"On three, boys," Will said. "A one, a two, a three!"

And so they sang their first death song since being cut from the gallows. Blue listened intently, wincing here and there from the gruesome detail in which the three musicians rendered the horrendous tortures Edwin "Full-Split" Grover would succumb to over night. Each would take a verse, outdoing the vile depictions from the previous singer. Skin flaying, bloodshed, broken bones, severed appendages.

Once they were done, Blue shook his head, pondering how these three could think of such things. The musicians smiled brightly, proud of the imagery they shared through song. "That," Blue said, "was indescribably awful. Almost too awful for the likes of Edwin."

"Almost," Rojo said.

"But nothing's too bad for a piece of horse shit like Edwin," Will added. "Good riddance."

Joseph stared toward a window with haunted eyes, as if he had a cross to bear and the weight threatened to take him down.

Blue crossed the room and pulled a bottle from a cupboard. "What do you say we have a drink? After that rendition, I need one."

"I've never seen a drink I turned down," Rojo said.

After scaring up several coffee cups and a couple of shot glasses, Blue and the Bridgeford Trio toasted to the death of Edwin Grover. They had several drinks afterward, chatting and sharing stories through the night until they became tired.

Tomorrow there was going to be a showdown.

CHAPTER TWENTY

SCREAMS IN THE NIGHT

MINNIE AWOKE TO A series of agonized screams from within the walls of Covington Ranch. Awash in sweat, her skin felt cold and sticky. The screams came again. She got out of bed, slipped on a nightgown, grabbed her gun, and went to seek out the source of the noise.

It came from Edwin's room. Minnie opened the door to find a horror show.

The sheets had been pulled from the bed, leaving Edwin lying on the feather mattress, which was awash in blood, reminding Minnie of the bed Thomas lay in nearby. Edwin's screams stretched out in long agonized wails. His eyelids had been ripped off, causing his eyes to protrude in an almost comic manor that was equally grotesque, mainly because he couldn't close them. His eyes danced wildly, but he didn't seem to be registering much. Minnie moved to his aid, thinking that someone must have snuck in and tortured him, but then things began happening to his body as if an invisible intruder, someone equally as demented as Edwin, was at work with a knife. His eyebrows were sliced of and flung to the floor. His ears came off next. His screams came in ear-bleeding pitch, high and dripping with terror and pain. Strips of flesh came off his arms as if at the blade of a sharpened razor. More screams. Edwin's jaw was pried open and his teeth extracted, one at a time, until his maw was nothing but bloody gums, after which his tongue emerged as if being pulled, and was then severed and flung in the pile, after which he began choking on the blood collecting in this throat, bubbling like a cauldron.

Minnie watched in horror, transfixed. There was no one in the room, and yet Edwin was being ripped apart, piece by piece. And there was nothing she could do. She was afraid if she intervened she too would be attacked by . . . whatever it was that did this.

Edwin's face was almost stripped to the bone. His head lolled to the side, eyes staring off, unable to close. Blood ran off his face onto the mattress, saturating it in deep red. One by one his fingers were severed and tossed onto the pile. Every single one of them. Next his toes, though not as neatly as his finger, as they were pulled until the bones snapped and the flesh ripped. His screams grew hoarse as he continued choking on blood that shot out of his destroyed mouth in random geysers. The long johns he wore to sleep were pulled down, and that's when his manhood was extracted. At this, Minnie cringed and reared back. The bloody mess of meat from between his legs, shreds of tissue and veins dangling like wet threads from a damaged garment, was thrown onto the pile.

At this point Edwin breathed deep breaths, quick and sharp as his body jerked and shuddered out a death rattle. How he could remain conscious after so much torture and blood loss was a true anomaly. It was as if he were being kept alive so that he was forced to endure the destruction of his body.

Finally, his long knife rose from the floor beside his bead, as if being guided by an invisible hand. The blade came down on his sternum and made a quick slash across his belly to his ruined pelvis. With a burst of painful screams and groans, his stomach tore open in a splash of blood and bile. His insides lurched from his body, piling themselves on the floor. After this act of brutality, Edwin took his last breath.

Minnie watched from the hall, terrified that whatever got Edwin would come for her. She didn't believe in ghosts or the supernatural, but there was no explanation for what she just witnessed.

What happened next was beyond vile, something that would haunt Minnie. The pile of guts, fingers, toes, and flesh shuffled around on the floor, as if by unseen hands. A loop of intestine here, a few fingers there, the tongue, some teeth. Minnie watched as words were formed.

EDWIN FULL-SPLIT GROVER

Minnie stood there staring at the words on the floor for several minutes before she removed herself from the room of horrors. She padded down the hall, trembling. There was no explanation for what she had witnessed. Some invisible being had to have been in there, tearing Edwin apart.

Though the house was warm from the adobe that had soaked up the day's sun, Minnie felt chill. She wrapped herself in a quilt and sat in the front parlor trying to decipher what had just happened. Her mind kept coming back to the message in the floor. It was very much like the message Edwin had made for Blue. The one James had delivered.

That goddamned James, walking out on us like that. I'll kill him if ever I see him again.

After contemplating the message further, Minnie decided that Blue was behind this. He was sending *her* a message. He did it in a similar fashion to the Thomas message to make sure she knew who sent it. What she couldn't figure out was how the hell he'd done that to Edwin. If Blue was versed in the ways of black magic, getting revenge wasn't going to be as easy as Minnie had hoped.

She decided that she had to make her move, and fast.

CHAPTER TWENTY-ONE

THE SHOWDOWN

BLUE WAS UP EARLY. He hadn't slept all that well, what with wondering whether the death song worked or not. If so, he figured Minnie would be fit to burst. He fully expected things to escalate.

Eventually Will woke along with the others.

Blue made a big pot of dark coffee for everyone to share. His first words to Will were, "How do we know the death song worked?"

Will sipped his coffee and grimaced. "That's as black as a moonless night, Blue. You tryin' to kill us?"

Blue didn't respond.

"The death songs always work," Will said. "Edwin is as good as dead."

"You got a lot of faith in that there spell book," Blue said.

"Sure we do. That there book is the reason we're alive. Just so long as the notes are true, the spells work every time. Well, that and following the rules of the spells."

"Can anyone sing those songs and use the spells?"

Will nodded. "We didn't write the book. I figure we was just messing around with it and we realized that there was real to life magic. Anyone could have gotten the book and done the same."

"I wonder how many others there are out there."

"Books like this? I don't know. I've never seen another, I know that."

After downing the last of his cup of coffee, Blue said, "I have to visit Louise. I have a feeling things are going to go . . . full-split today. After the message we sent I wouldn't be surprised to see Minnie burst into town guns a blazing. You have one of my guns. Someone breaks in that door, shoot first, don't even bother asking questions. Someone knocks on it, don't say a word. I'll be back shortly."

"It's no problem," Rojo said. "There's three of us and one of her. I kinda like those odds."

"We think it's one of her," Blue said. "I don't know how many people she has up there. We'll be lucky if it's just one of her."

Blue left and headed for Louise's place. She must have sensed his arrival, for the door was open and she was waiting at the threshold.

"And what do I owe the pleasure, Blue Covington?"

"I just wanted to see you, that's all."

"Come in."

He followed her into her parlor and when she turned, he took her in his embrace. She accepted him and they kissed.

"I'm glad you're back," she said. "In town, I mean."

"Me too."

"I wasn't sure what the future held for me. I might be able to read other people's palms, but when I put my hands together I get nothing. I'd hoped you would come back, but I was beginning to consider my options."

"Well, I'm here now."

She paused and looked down, as if in shame.

"What's wrong?" Blue asked.

Louise swallowed hard. "It's just, you know the paper you gave me, the one with the music on it?"

Blue nodded.

"I apologize, I really do, but I was looking at it last night over the hearth and it slipped out of my hands. Fell right into the fire. I feel terrible, Blue. I hope the song is replaceable. It seemed to mean so much to you. I have to admit, I was kind of surprised to find you so eager to learn how to sing."

Blue thought on it for a moment, stoic poker face revealing absolutely nothing of his emotions in the matter. "You know what, it really doesn't matter." He took a deep breath and shook his head. "Turns out I didn't need to learn that song anyway. Louise, I want to ask you something."

She looked up, eyes wide. "Go ahead. I'm listening."

He dug into his pocket and pulled out a small wrapping of handkerchief embroidered in gold and silver. He unwrapped it and produced a ring. "This here is Momma's wedding ring. She gave it to me after Poppa died, told me to hold onto it until I met The One. Well, Louise, you're The One. Now, I have a feeling that there's gonna be a gunfight today. I have a feeling I'm going to be on the winning end of said gunfight, but there are no guarantees. I also know that this will be my last gunfight. I'm settling down here in La Plateau, on the ranch, and I would like for you to take my hand in marriage and join me."

Louise beamed, "Oh, Blue, you know I will!" She held out her hand, and Blue placed the ring on her finger, careful that his flesh didn't touch hers.

"Now, you can't keep that ring on that finger until we have a right proper ceremony. We can do it at the church."

"I love you, Blue Covnington," she said, taking Blue into her arms.

"I love you too."

It wasn't too long after Blue left to see Louise that Minnie showed up. Days ago Edwin had told her which room was Blue's. When he'd kidnapped Thomas he'd walked right into the lobby and found it empty, slipped behind the front desk and looked at the ledger. Easy as pie.

At the door, Minnie wielded a shotgun she'd had custom made in Louisville, Kentucky. It had a cylindrical chamber, like on a revolver, that held six slugs. She stood for a moment gathering her courage and working through her plan. Wasn't much of a plan. Go inside and take care of business. She hoped she was early enough to catch Blue off guard. If there were any others in the room, she'd shoot them first. She didn't want to hesitate with Blue too much, but on the other hand she wanted to damn well make sure he knew why she was killing him. Wouldn't do no good to just off the man without him knowing why. That wouldn't sit well with Minnie.

Her adrenalin rose, and a few moments later she kicked in the door, which wasn't very difficult considering it had been kicked in a few days ago and only hastily repaired. She launched into the room, shotgun at the ready. What she found were three men, none of them Blue Covington. What happened next, happened fast.

One of them said, "Oh shit, it's her!" He grabbed for something that was resting in his lap. Minnie didn't hesitate. She marched forward and pulled the trigger, launching a slug into Will's face before he could lift the gun and have a shot at her. She then shifted to the right and popped a slug through Joseph's chest, and then shifted to the left plugging Rojo with a slug, right in the face, so close the back of his cranium exploded onto the wall like somebody beat the hell out of a bunch of pomegranates. Joseph gasped for breath, so Minnie put the shotgun to his forehead and launched his brains on the adjoining wall. The slug plowing through his head, piercing the wall right in the middle of the bloody brain painting.

"Blue Covington!" Minnie called out. "Come out, come out!"

No response. She searched the room, but he wasn't there. She went to the door she'd kicked in and carefully scanned the hallway, fearing that someone would be coming due to the blasts of her shotgun, but for now it was clear. She closed the door and resigned to a corner to wait.

Blue was on his way up the stairs of the hotel when he heard the gunshots. He stopped, counting them as they exploded above. Four total, and none of them from the gun he left with Will. Sounded like a large caliber—perhaps slugs from a shotgun—but didn't sound like the shooter had time to reload. Even with a double barrel there would have had to be one reload, and Blue specifically heard the first three shots in immediate succession. Could mean more than one shooter.

He took the stairs up and hung back at the landing. Peeking around the edge he saw that the door to his room was wide open. He pulled back, and considered what his next move would be. Moments later he heard the door close. Another peak around the corner confirmed this.

Footsteps came from below. The hotel owner emerged. "What's the ruckus? Sounded like gunfire."

"It was," Blue said. "But it's nothing you need to trifle with. Something I have to deal with. I assure you, any damages will be paid for. I know that door's been kicked in a time or two."

"Should I call the sheriff?"

Blue made a snorting sound. "Hiriam? The hell he gonna do?" Blue shook his head. "No, this is personal. I have to fight my own battles. If I were you I'd go down and sit behind that desk of yours. You're gonna hear gunfire. You want to call on the sheriff, you go ahead and do so after that."

The hotel owner looked perplexed, but he heeded Blue's advice and descended the stairs to the lobby where he positioned himself behind the front desk, trembling as he listened for gunfire.

Blue took to the hallway, slow and careful as not to step on the creaky spots he'd made note of as he came to and from his room over the last week since he'd been there. At the door he pulled his revolver. At this point the door wasn't even latching, the wood having been splintered away from a couple of good kicks.

He had no idea how many people were in there. He figured Minnie was there for sure, but did she bring back up? Had the death song worked, or was that crazy bastard Edwin in there, ready to go all full-split?

There was only one way to find out.

Palming the door, Blue merely pushed and it swung open on dry, squealing hinges in dire need of oil. He pointed his revolver into the room, but didn't see anyone. He walked in, slowly, and there she was, tucked into a corner and wielding one goddamned big shotgun the likes of which Blue had never seen before. And she had the thing pointed at him.

"So we finally meet," Blue said, revolver trained on her forehead.

"Indeed. I been waitin' a long time for this." Minnie's face was clenched in an angry grimace. "What you did cannot be repented, and therefore I have to kill you."

"It didn't happen way you think."

"The hell it didn't!" she spat her words at him. "I know what happened. I saw the bodies." Her scowl deepened. "My family. All shot up. It was you went to get my brother, to get his bounty, and you done shot up my entire family like some savage." She shook her head. "I didn't even think a bounty hunter was that cold hearted."

"See, things didn't go like what you heard. Truth is, your brother killed your family. Did it right before my eyes. I was gonna take Jimbo in alive if I could, but when he went and killed everybody in the room, I was forced to kill him before he pointed that gun at me."

Minnie thought on this for a half a second and then said, "I don't believe you. You're a liar. A killer of children, of innocent people."

Blue gripped his gun tight, finger on the hair trigger. The look in Minnie's eyes was that of a woman gone mad. There was nothing Blue could say that would convince her of the truth. She had her mind made up.

From the hallway a creak in the floorboards disturbed the tense silence. Both Blue and Minnie's weapons went off.

Both of them were hit.

The blast from the slug knocked Blue across the room. It hit his right shoulder, tearing through the flesh and just about severing his arm. His gun went flying. He scrambled for purchase, fearing that she would come up with that monstrosity of a gun and blow his face clean off like she'd done to two of the Bridgeford Trio, but there was no other sound in the room.

Blue sat himself up, gritting his teeth from the excruciating pain that emanated from his destroyed right shoulder. Minnie's body lay motionless on the ground. He did his best to crawl to her. His aim had been true. A bullet hole pierced her forehead. She'd died instantly.

Blue surveyed the room. The musicians were in a bad way. She'd done them dirty, blasting their brains all over the walls. Blue felt awful for them. He'd grown to like them, regardless of what they'd done to La Plateau. Being in such close quarters with them had been an exercise in redemption.

He managed to stand. With every movement pain radiated from his shoulder, traveling down his body like jolts of electricity. Gritting his teeth, he walked across the room and over Minnie's body to a window. He tried to open it, but it was stuck, as windows in old hotels often were. He didn't even think about what he was doing when he kicked the glass. It shattered easily enough, raining down in front of the hotel. Blue reached his head out between the tooth-like jagged maw of the window. "Louise! Louise!"

Below, a pair of kids playing in the street saw Blue. "We'll get her!" they yelled, and then they were off.

A voice came from behind. "Are you all—?"

Blue turned to see Grant, the hotel manager, standing in the doorway to the room, his face white like a cloud. His mouth gaped as he took in the tableau. Four bodies on the ground. Bloody brains splattered on the wall. Bullet holes here and there, and Blue taking a seat, his right arm swinging limp as if it were only attached to his body by mere tendons.

"Please," Blue said. "Get something to wrap around my arm."

"Oh my lord. I've . . . I've."

"Quickly!"

Blue sucked air through tightly clenched teeth. He couldn't bear to look at his arm.

Grant rushed into the room and pulled a knife from his belt. He cut a strip off the bed linens and assisted in wrapping it around Blue's arm, blood soaking into it faster than he could wrap.

"It's bad," Blue said. "I'm loosing a lot of blood."

Footsteps echoed from down the hall, growling louder, and then Louise was there. She stopped at the doorway, took in the scene, and then saw that Blue had been injured and rushed to his aid.

"My God, Blue, what happened?"

"She shot me in the shoulder with a slug."

"It looks awful bad." Louise looked at Grant. "Go send for a doctor, and get the sheriff while you're at it."

"I've already sent for the sheriff," he said, as if he'd done a great deed.

"Well go after a doctor. He's losing a lot of blood."

"Okay, okay. I'll be back."

Grant left. Blue said, "That book, over there on the tea table. Grab it."

Hesitantly, Louise grabbed the book. She studied the cover before opening it.

"Find the Health Song. Or better yet, find a healing song. Something like that."

Flipping through the pages Louise regarded the book quizzically. Mumbling the titles of the songs as she went, and then she came across a familiar one. The resurrection song. She paused, glanced at Blue whose eyes were closed, teeth clenched tight, clearly in pain. She dismissed the song, flipping pages, looking for anything that had to do with health, but she couldn't help but wonder what it was Blue had wanted with resurrection.

"Nothing?" Blue asked, his voice strained in agony. "I'm losing blood. Feeling weak. I don't think I can make it 'til a doctor gets here, and even then I don't know a doctor here in La Plateau can help me. Probably cut off the arm and cauterize the stump, and then I have infection to worry about."

"How else are you going to get help? I don't understand what I'm looking for."

"That book. Keep looking. There's bound to be some kind of health or healing song."

Another several minutes of searching, song after song—Love Song, Rain Song, Crops Song, Friendship Song, Hunting Song—before she came across the healing song.

"I've found it!" Louise said.

"Good. All you have to do is sing it to me. Note for note. Think you can do that? Also, I don't know for sure, but I think you have to think of me while you're singing it, and use my name in the song."

"Use your name in the song," she whispered as she read the lyrics and familiarized herself with the notes. "Ah, I see. Just give me a few seconds to make sure I know all the notes."

Her eyes drifted away from the page as she hummed the melody. Looking closer at the three dead men scattered on the floor, the song titles she'd just skimmed through danced in her mind. She hadn't seen it in the book, but understood where the death song had come from.

"Blue! Those are the musicians who were hanged."

"Don't worry about that. I'm dying here. Trust me. That book will heal me. Just read the song, note for note, and think about me while you're doing it. I promise you, it will work better than a small town physician. That damn doctor's hardly worth a shit anyways."

Pulling in a deep breath, Louise began singing the song. Her voice was crystalline and perfect, which was much nicer on the ears than the Bridgeford Trio, who were good singers, but more of a variety act. Blue could get used to having Louise sing to him. She sung the words, improvising Blue's name into the song a few times, all the while thinking about having him in good health. Thinking about their future together as husband and wife.

After reading every lyric and hitting every note, she put the book down, careful to leave it open to the healing song. She watched Blue silently for a moment before saying anything. He was still in pain, wincing and closing his eyes tight, sucking air through his teeth.

"How do we know it worked?" she asked.

"Give it a few more minutes."

Those minutes were tense. Louise hoped for the doctor, but he didn't show. Despite having seen the destruction that the death songs had caused, she wasn't entirely sure what she'd sung was going to heal Blue.

But then, Blue stretched out his damaged arm and began opening and closing his hand, flexing his muscles. The blood remained, soaked into the linens wrapping his arm. He used his other hand to unfurl the wrappings. His shoulder was awash in blood, but the wound had sealed itself.

"The pain's gone," Blue said. He smiled.

Louise knew Blue to be a fairly stoic man. Seeing him smile like this filled her heart with warmth and joy, even in a room with so many dead scattered across the floor.

"My God," she said. "It worked. It really worked."

Blue stood from his perch in the chair and drew Louise into a warm embrace. "I told you it would work." They kissed, and then were interrupted when Grant and David, the local physician, walked in.

Grant looked perplexed. He took his glasses off and put them back on, as if that would somehow change things. "But . . . but wasn't your arm . . .?"

"I can maybe explain later," Blue said, "but let's just say I've been healed. David, that's your name, if I remember correctly?" The doctor nodded. "Your service will not be necessary."

The doctor's eyes deepened. "Grant," he said, glaring at the hotel manager. "I was in a hot game of stud. I thought this was an emergency?"

Grant moved his lips open and closed, unsure of what to say, babbling this and that like he'd suffered some great trauma. He shook his head in confusion.

David calmed some and said, "Well, I'm just glad it wasn't a major medical emergency." He eyed the bodies on the floor. "Some gunfight you had in here." He squinted. "Hey, ain't them the fellas was hung some weeks back?"

Blue walked over to the doctor and put a hand on his back, gently ushering him to the door. He shook his head. "Naw. They were hung. What would they be doing here? No, these are some friends of mine. The lady is Minnie Granger. She killed them. Damn near killed me while she was at it."

"Dear lord, how tragic. Well, I'll send for the coroner. Four bodies is a lot in one day for a town like La Plateau."

"Not to worry. Tell him there's one body."

It was David's turn to be perplexed. "One body? I don't understand."

Blue snickered. "Don't worry about it. My friends, well, let's just say they're playing dead."

David tilted his head and tried to peek over Blue's shoulder, but Blue continued forward, ushering both David and Grant through the splintered doorframe.

After David left for the coroner and Grant went back downstairs to wait for the sheriff, Blue grabbed the book and flipped through the pages.

"What are you looking for?" Louise asked. "And what's all that talk about just one body?"

"You're gonna sing these boys a resurrection song."

"But these *are* the musicians who done killed half the town, right?"

"Right. I had trouble with that too, but they've helped me out a lot. With Minnie gone, the ranch is mine again. And I'm not sure I could have done it without them. Ah, here it is." Blue handed over the book. "Sing it for Will first.

He's the fella in the middle. I don't know we can sing it for all three at once or individually or what. He says there are rules to the songs. Some, like the death song, can only be used once in a day, for instance."

Louise was reluctant. "But after what they did to La Plateau?"

"They regret their actions, Louise. Don't you believe in redemption? Forgiveness?"

"That's a lot to forgive, Blue."

"I know. Please, do it for me. I owe them this."

She hesitated some more, then said, "His name is Will?"

"Yes. He comes back, he can take care of the rest."

"I'm only doing this because I love you. Do you understand that, Blue Covington?"

Blue smiled for the second time that day. "And I love you too, soon-to-be Louise Covington."

That made her smile back, despite the fact that she was about to raise the dead. "Well, here goes." She took in a deep breath and began to sing the resurrection song with a murderer named Will on her mind.

After she sung the song, she watched Will, fascinated and horrified to see him come back.

"This is the second time Will's been brought back from the dead in under a week," Blue said.

"Second time?"

"I killed him the first time."

"Is that so?"

"I was upset what they did to Cort. That was the last death song. Well, the last one had anything to do with our people."

Louise nodded. "Well, at least you got to kill him. That makes me feel a little bit better, I suppose."

A few moments later Will coughed and came to. "Where the hell am I?" he said, just like last time.

"You've been brought back from the dead," Blue said. "Again."

Will blinked his eyes into focus, and then noticed his friends to the left and right of him, their heads destroyed like rotten watermelons bashed with sticks. He looked at his hands, all covered in blood, and tried to wipe them on his shirt, only to find that too was soaked through in red.

"Lordy, lordy, we got us into a bad one, didn't we?"

Blue nodded. "It was Minnie. She come in here while I was away. I guess you're not the sharpest shooter in the bunch. You didn't even get a shot off at her."

The gun still lay in Will's lap. "I never was a quick draw."

"We didn't know if we should sing the resurrection song for everybody. Figured you know the rules, you can take it from here."

Will hung his head. "I can't look at them. It's too much. And there's nothing I can do." He sighed. "Like the death song, the resurrection song can only be used once in a day. We'd sung it once everyday for the whole group wile hanging on the gallows. You can sing it for more than one person like that. Tomorrow will be too late. They'll have been dead for too long. You don't want to use that song on someone's been dead too long. The results are . . . ghastly."

Blue knelt down and put his hand on Will's shoulder. "I'm sorry."

Will nodded. "Thanks. I've been with them boys for going on . . . a hundred years." He let out a sigh. "We've had some close calls, but," he looked at the book, open to the resurrection song, "that book has saved our asses on many an occasion." Will reached over and grabbed the book, closing it. He handed it to Blue, who took it, uncertain what was happening. "I want you to have it. Joseph brought it into the fold, and we used the hell out of it, not always for good. I think I want to take on the rest of my life without depending on these damn songs." He offered a weak smile. "I mean, I have several memorized, but who knows how long I'll remember them. The life song is a good one first thing in the morning." His face deepened. "I'll be sure to forget that damned death song. I have no use for that." He looked Blue in the eyes, and then looked Louise in the eyes. "I want the both of you to know that I am deeply sorry for what we did to your town. I know Rojo and Joseph ain't a fair trade for the men and woman we killed, but . . ."

"We'll take this book for good keeping," Blue said. "Look, you'd better go. The townspeople find you here, they'll hang you again. You run out yonder, follow the trail we took to Covington Ranch. You go ahead and take one of my horses. Go sing songs for people. Get a couple new musicians. But if I get word that you been using them death songs, I'll come out of retirement and hunt you down whether there's a bounty out for you or not. Hear me?"

"Loud and clear." Will thrust out his hand, Blue accepted and they shook heartily. "Thank you, Blue. You're a truly decent man. Perhaps the most decent I've ever run across, and I've been around for at least two lifetimes." Will smirked, bristling his moustache, and then left the hotel.

Blue and Louise waited for the authorities, which turned out to be Frenchy Hill, unofficial mayor of town, and the coroner, who was only prepared for one body.

EPILOGUE

IT TOOK SEVERAL WEEKS to get the Covington Ranch back in shape.

Thomas had been killed. He'd been brutally tortured for days before someone hammered railroad ties into his head. He was given a proper burial right there on the ranch in the family plot.

Edwin was found lying atop a feather mattress that was so soaked in drying blood it had become a thick slab of solidifying jelly. His body had become fused to the blood-jelly mattress. He was given a less dignified send off to the ever after by way of funeral pyre, right there on the ranch. With a bit of kerosene he went up like dry tinder, mattress and all.

Both bedrooms had to be remodeled, especially Edwin's, considering the message in guts and body parts that was left to rot into the hardwood. Blue did much of the work, hiring help from town. He bartered, but most folks offered their labor for free, happy that things were getting back to normal, and thankful that Blue had saved La Plateau.

Several months later Blue and Louise were married. The wedding happened at the church in town. Just about everyone in La Plateau attended. It was a wonderful ceremony that seemed to bring the town together, much needed in the wake of so much tragedy. There was dancing, drink, and music . . . not from a vocal trio.

They hired a few ranch hands, but Blue missed old Cort "Pappy" Rudgers. The new guys did a good enough job, but Blue figured old Pappy would have put them to shame were he still alive.

Louise continued her palm reading business, though on a part-time schedule. She sold her apartment and opened up in a little shop in the middle of town, by appointment only.

On cool nights, such as tonight, Blue and Louise enjoyed sitting in the glider they had built for the front porch, sipping tea and looking up at the stars.

"I have a little confession to make," Louise said.

"Oh?"

She nodded. Blue could see in her body language that it wasn't something overly important. Louise continued, "You remember when you were trying to get me to help you learn how to sing that song? That resurrection song?"

"Sure do. We didn't get far with that, did we?"

"No, sir, we didn't. And I'll tell you why."

"You said your voice was all blown out or something. And you accidentally dropped the song into the hearth."

"I lied. I sung just fine up in your hotel room. You remember that? How could I sing if I'd damaged my vocals?"

Blue scrunched his face. "So why'd you lie to me?"

"Something about that song rubbed me wrong. It just didn't seem right. What were you going to do with it anyway?"

Blue sipped his tea and thought a moment. "I wanted to bring momma back." He paused, then added, "Just so I could talk to her one more time."

"Oh, Blue." Louise put her hand on his knee. "That would have been a bad idea. You remember what Will said. Just one day after his friends died and it would have been too late for that song to work . . . properly."

Blue nodded. "It was a bad idea, I'll confess to that. But I did get to see momma again. You did that for me. I didn't need the damn song anyways. All I needed was you."

"I'm glad I could do that for you."

Blue had tucked the song spell book up high on a book-shelf and forgot about it. He was glad Will didn't have it anymore, but uncertain that the world even needed such magic. But as much as Louise tried to get him to burn the thing, he wouldn't.

Deep down, he figured it would come in handy one day.

ABOUT THE AUTHOR

Robert Essig is the author of over twenty books including This Damned House, Baby Fights, and Broth House. He has published over 100 short stories and edited three small press anthologies. His anthology Chew on This! was nominated for a Splatterpunk Award. Robert lives with his family in East Tennessee.